Lizy J Campbell

Lapis

Lapis- Lizy J Campbell 2ND edition
Copyright © 2024. All rights reserved.

ALL RIGHTS RESERVED: No part of this book may be reproduced, stored, or transmitted, in any form, without the express and prior permission in writing of The Elite Lizzard Publishing Company or the author. This book may not be circulated in any form of binding or cover other than that in which it is currently published.

This book is licensed for your personal enjoyment only. All rights are reserved. The author or Publisher does not grant you rights to resell or distribute this book without prior written consent of the copyright owner of this book. This book must not be copied, transferred, sold, or distributed in any way.

Disclaimer: Neither The Elite Lizzard Publishing Company nor authors will handle repercussions to anyone who utilizes the subject of this book for illegal, immoral, or unethical use.

This is a work of fiction. The views expressed herein do not necessarily reflect those of the publisher.

This book or part thereof may not be reproduced in any form, stored in a retrieval system, or transmitted in any form by any means-electronic, mechanical, photocopy, recording or otherwise-without prior written consent of the publisher, except as provided by Canada copyright law.

Published by The Elite Lizzard Publishing Company

CHAPTER 1

Drops of perspiration adorned Ruby's brow like glistening beaded jewels as she hacked her way through the dense grass of Nosy Mangabe. It was an island nestled just off the coast of Madagascar. The machete on loan, but keen enough to rival a barber's razor, sliced through the vegetation easily, unveiling a path that promised to lead her to the buried, preordained gem.

Unlike the sunny affluent life that she knew in California, where sand and wealth shielded her from broken nails, Ruby found herself on the cusp of a thrilling adventure. At the tender age of 20, she boasted a petite yet alluring silhouette, adorned with chocolate-brown hair and eyes that mirrored the hue of her namesake—red, a shade visible only to those who shared her bloodlines. To others, her eyes appeared hazel.

Ruby's existence to date had been cocooned in financial comfort, thanks to her parents. However, the journey from the shore to her current location had been anything but luxurious.

The dusty, jolting ride through the rugged back roads of the island, aboard an ancient rusty rattling jeep, had set the tone and mood since getting off the long flight. Intrigue hung in the air as Ruby pressed forward.

Amidst the untamed beauty of thick, overgrown greenery, Ruby's guide, Andry, didn't speak much, and not willingly offering any information as to how long this trip was going to be. He was no stranger to her family, having crossed paths with her Aunt Safire years ago on a similar quest that Ruby was now undertaking.

Equipped with a birthday book and a plane ticket, Ruby's purpose on the island unfolded like the pages of her gifted guidebook. This precious gem, a birthstone and birthright, held significance for every member of her family upon reaching adulthood.

As Ruby wielded her machete through the thick grass, impatience crept in. "Andry, how much farther to the location? This is proving to be more work than I expected," she exclaimed, brushing off grass from her once pristine jeans.

Andry, swatting away buzzing insects, warned, "Your journey has just begun, Miss.

There's more to this than just a quick trip, one must ponder life at this time."

Rolling her eyes at his cryptic message, Ruby retorted, "It better not be. You promised a short trip on the phone—here and there and done, remember?"

Andry persisted, "Have you delved into the journal? Dates are crucial, and your aunt's experience may offer valuable insights."

Ruby dismissed his concern, "I was too excited for my inheritance to study it. Besides, with modern technology and Google, this should be a breeze. You do know what that is I hope?"

"Yes, miss, we have this back at the office." Andry rolled his eyes while looking away.

The three men behind them, carrying the supplies in the back, snickered at Andry's comment.

Andry, wiping sweat from his brow, emphasized, "Out here, there is no internet. We must proceed cautiously."

As the sun began its descent, Andry suggested, "Miss, I think we should stop and set up camp for the night, it's getting later into the evening and the crew needs to set up camp to prepare food and the tents. Rest assured, however; we will have you there in no time." The guide surveyed the area to find a flat spot of land and pointed to the crew to set up camp.

Ruby, exhausted but enamored by the breathtaking sunset, acquiesced. The vibrant hues of the sky and the lush greenery of Nosy Mangabe left her in awe.

Having been on planes, boats, and jeeps, Ruby found herself at the campsite, where memories of her flight attendant Donna's unsolicited honeymoon advice echoed in her mind. One of the helpers started on dinner amidst a freshly started crackling fire. Lost in the thoughts of the day she noticed that the tents were up.

Ruby was tapped on the shoulder, which caused her to mutter, "I must have been daydreaming."

"Come, sit." The helper was an older gentleman, with thin white hair, a deep-set of crow's feet lines around his eyes, and a gorgeous caramel color tan.

The food was delicious, pink rice with cashews and scallions. For dessert: Mofo Akondro; which translated in English, banana fritters.

Ruby ate to her satisfaction and became increasingly curious about her aunt's time here. "So, tell me Andry, when you were a guide for my aunt, did she have an easy time of it here?"

Andry finished swallowing his fritter and smiled with crumbs around his mouth, "She was how you say, an outdoor type."

Ruby laughed and picked another fritter up, "Ah, okay, was it easy for her to locate, her inheritance?"

Andry's facial expression changed to a more serious tone, "Well, at first she was much like you, seemed to be busy, just very busy. She's in a rush. She wanted to come, to find, and go. she never thinks that she be here for a long time, much like you. I tell her, as I tell you, that things take time. But for her, she more concerned for the ending."

Ruby felt like there was something she wasn't quite grasping when he spoke. She considered; it must just be due to the language barrier.

Andry spoke to the other men in Malagasy, his native tongue. Ruby felt slightly put out, since she didn't understand a word of it, and thought speaking another language in front of someone who didn't speak it, was rude.

"Sorry for that, those other men don't speak English as well as me, so I have to tell them the plans in the morning. That way, they will know what to do."

It was as if he read her thoughts.

She brushed it off as coincidence and began to yawn. It was nightfall and aside from the fire, the stars were out, and the sky was clear.

It was an amazing view, since Ruby lived in the city she never saw the sky so full of stars twinkling so brightly in the night sky. She felt contented with her full stomach and sleepy daze, as she stared up into the heavens.

"Will there be any creatures I should worry about while I am sleeping?" Ruby yawned as she spoke.

"A lot miss, your tent is here, next to mine, you must keep it closed at night no matter if you get hot. There are many things awake at night here and would like to crawl in."

"Ah, that's reassuring." She now felt the need for sleep and was too tired to worry about it.

She got up, slipped into the tent with an inviting bed already made for her, which looked to be a very fine quality and it was calling her name. She didn't even change her clothes. As soon as her head hit the pillow, she was out for the night.

CHAPTER 2

The next morning, Ruby appeared from her tent drenched in sweat as the scorching sun threatened to burn through the fabric. Imagining herself as an unwilling ant under a giant magnifying glass, she hastily changed and flung open the tent, desperate for air.

Andry and the other men had already put the tents away and had coffee and sweet rice cakes waiting for her for breakfast.

Ruby looked around and suddenly felt as though she might have slept in and was delaying the trip. "What time is it?"

"It's 7:30 am, miss," he sipped on his coffee.

"Oh, I thought I had overslept since everything is packed and ready to go."

"No, no, this is how we do things; we keep how you say; tidy. Plus, it is what your family is paying us for.

"Tidy works, yes, or organized." Ruby couldn't help correcting his grammar.

By now, the intense sun and the humidity from the dense wildlife made it just barely tolerable to breathe. Andry and the men had no problems, it seemed. Ruby on the other hand, was about to keel over, when one of the men started shouting something.

Andry turned around and saw Ruby's cheeks flushed red and quickly gave her some water from his flask. "I see you are not used to this heat miss; this is not going to be pleasant for you."

"Well, it's no air-conditioned office like I am used to, that's for sure."

Andry laughed. "No ma'am, no air conditioners, unless you at a resort."

One of the men yelled something and all the men at once dropped the bags and looked up into the trees.

Ruby didn't have time to ask what was going on, when Andry quickly grabbed her arm and started escorting her, speed walking to a cave that appeared out of nowhere.

"What's happening?" Ruby was out of breath.

Andry whispered, "A black cat is in the trees."

"What?... a cat?" Ruby was perplexed.

He looked her in the eyes, "The black panthers rule these parts of the jungle. It hides high above the trees, waiting for its prey to walk by. It then pounces on unsuspecting animals and humans alike. My men are distracting it so I can get you to safety. It won't come in this cave because it doesn't need trouble from the animals that live and sleep inside."

"Umm, what animals sleep in here?" Ruby's heart skipped a beat.

"Gorillas, very large ones, they come in here at night when the heat is too much to bare, or if there is a tropical storm." He flicked on the flashlight as they reached total darkness. "Stay close, if they haven't gone, I will use a flare to scare them off."

Ruby, who had never come face to face with either of those animals, suddenly felt like coming here was a mistake.

The temperature inside the cave was cooler and the air was not as dense. Andry flashed the light on all corners of the cave to make sure they were alone. The only thing to be seen was the glistening of white bones reflected by the flashlight.

Ruby decided to check the journal and see the whereabouts of the location of the jewel she had come to claim. "Andry, can you shine the light on my journal? I want to see where we are sup-posed to be looking for it in this cave."

"Miss this is not the right cave, the one we need is near the other side of the island. This one is just one of them. You can get lost looking in these caves if you don't know the way. You can die here too." Andry's voice broke a little with emotion as he spoke.

"Are you serious? Jeez. Do you know of someone who has? I am sorry I shouldn't pry."

Andry sighed deeply, "Yes it's ok to ask. Many who come here just think it's a honeymoon destination. They never think of the dangers. They often get bored in resorts and decide to wander off. A couple last year was viciously attacked by a panther. They were found partially eaten. But we keep this quiet, and we pay the media, so it doesn't get out. Please keep this to yourself miss I beg of you; tourism is how we feed our families here, so we need it to stay quiet. Your aunt knew the dangers even before those deaths, she could see through a lot of things. She was a gift to our island and did many wonderful things for us in which I hope in time you will come to understand."

Ruby didn't, but nodded quietly, "So, when will it be safe to venture out again so we can continue our journey?"

Andry sat on a rock and opened a box from his bag, "One of the men will yell into the cave to give us all clear but in the meantime, pop tart? We bring some American treats for you; do you like them? I love these things."

"No thanks I don't eat processed foods."

Andry laughed. "Suit yourself."

Suddenly, the air grew tense as a low rumble echoed through the darkness beyond the inside of the cave. The flickering flashlight revealed the hulking figures of gorillas. Massive and imposing, the primates stirred from their slumber, their eyes reflecting an unexpected and unsettling curiosity. Ruby's heart raced, realizing the precariousness of their situation. Andry, displaying a calm demeanor born of familiarity with these creatures, slowly retreated, guiding Ruby back into the shadows.

"That was too close for comfort Andry." Ruby was starting to feel the weight of danger exploring in the wild.

"You are safe with me; I will not let anything happen to you on my watch I can assure you." Andry took out another pop tart unphased by what he just saw.

"Thank you."

CHAPTER 3

The men persisted in their relentless shouts, their voices cutting through the thick jungle foliage like a desperate plea. The tangled web of slippery leaves and rough vines obscured their vision, adding an extra layer of challenge to the already daunting task of spotting the elusive black panther. The jungle floor, damp, and mossy, clung to their every step, making the pursuit even more treacherous.

Gaethon, positioned as the second in command, assumed leadership in Andry's absence. Though he harbored a command of broken English, he chose to keep to himself, his reluctance to engage with Ruby was clear. Despite finding her physically attractive, he couldn't shake an unease about her eyes, the fleeting glimmers of red that mirrored her gemstone's namesake.

As the trees rustled to his left, Gaethon crouched down, trying to discern the approaching presence. Before he could signal the other two men, a sudden and ominous stillness enveloped the jungle. The black devil panther, with its amber eyes gleaming like predatory beacons, struck swiftly and silently. Gaethon became the unfortunate victim, the panther's powerful muscles propelling it directly toward his throat. Almost invisible among the dark shadows of the savage jungle, the panther claimed its prey with ruthless efficiency.

The remaining two men, with utter terror etched across their faces, sprinted toward the safety of the cave as the panther dragged Gaethon away.

The beast's sinewy form disappeared into the dense foliage, its tail flicking in the air, signaling the inevitable culmination of primal instincts—consumption. The raw and unforgiving dance of life and death played out in the heart of the untamed wilderness, leaving behind a chilling reminder of what lurked in the lush veneer green jungles of Nosy Mangabe.

CHAPTER 4

Andry drank some water because the pop tarts he ate always made him thirsty. He was starting to worry why it has taken this long for Gaethon to give the all-clear.

The oppressive heat of the jungle seemed to intensify, each step inside the cave now echoing with the heaviness of an impending tragedy. Andry, who had ventured out to investigate the continued absence of Gaethon's all-clear signal, returned with a heaviness in his heart. The atmosphere shifted abruptly as the two men, normally boisterous and full of life, entered the cave like somber shadows. Their shouts and cries were replaced by an eerie silence that hung in the air, an unspoken revelation of something had gone terribly wrong.

Ruby's heart quickened as she saw Andry speaking with the men, his shoulders shaking with grief. She could feel the weight of the news before it was even uttered. Panic set in as she realized the size of the situation. Whatever had happened was nothing short of a nightmare. Andry, engulfed in his sorrow, shared a devastating truth.

"Miss, I must try to get you back. It is not safe to go on here without something to defend ourselves; we need a gun and more manpower," Andry confessed, the pain etched across his face.

Tears streamed down his cheeks, and Ruby was paralyzed with shock. The gravity of the situation hit her like a tidal wave. Andry's revelation shattered any illusions she had about the expedition. A son, a life, had been taken by the merciless jungle, and the weight of that loss hung heavy in the air.

"That man was my son, Gaethon, and that wicked devil took him from me today," Andry's voice quivered with grief, and Ruby's heart sank. The cave, once a haven of safety, now felt like a tomb of despair. Ruby, grappling with a sudden sense of guilt, couldn't help but blame herself for this tragedy. If only she hadn't embarked on this journey, if only her family's legacy wasn't veiled in cryptic intentions, Gaethon would still be alive. The tears flowed freely as she mourned not only for Gaethon but for the shattered remnants of what was supposed to be a quest for her family's birthright.

"I understand, please take me back, and I am so sorry for your son," Ruby managed to utter between sobs, her voice choked with grief. Andry, despite his own anguish, nodded in understanding. The journey, once filled with excitement and anticipation, now hung in limbo, suspended by the cruel hands of fate.

In the aftermath of this tragedy, the cave offered no solace. The walls, once mere observers of the expedition's unfolding drama, now bore witness to a sorrow that transcended words. Andry, after composing himself in the cocoon of grief and mourning, became the reluctant harbinger of a return journey.

As they retraced their steps through the dense jungle, the once-familiar surroundings now seemed like a maze of sorrow. The vibrant foliage, which had earlier beckoned with the promise of discovery, now concealed the harsh reality of the untamed wilderness. The sounds of the jungle, once a symphony of life, now seemed eerily muted.

In the hushed trek back, Ruby found herself grappling with a profound sense of loss and regret.

Gaethon's absence, a void in the expedition's fabric, echoed the unpredictable brutality that lurked within the heart of Nosy Mangabe. She couldn't shake the feeling that her pursuit of a family jewel had led to an irreparable fracture in the lives of those who had once been her guides.

Back at the campsite, the remnants of their expedition lay in stark contrast to the first fervor. Tents that once promised shelter now seemed like mere symbols of transience. The fire, once a source of warmth and camaraderie, now flickered in somber silence.

Andry, burdened by the weight of grief, addressed Ruby with a solemn determination. "Miss, we'll make our way back to the shore. I'll arrange for a boat to take you back to where you came from." His gaze, haunted by the recent loss, held a silent plea for understanding.
Ruby, her eyes swollen from tears, nodded in agreement.

As they embarked on the journey back to the shore, the dense jungle began to release its grip on them. The sounds of the wilderness, though still ominous, carried a sense of farewell. Each step echoed a silent requiem for Gaethon, a soul claimed by the unforgiving heart of Nosy Mangabe.

The boat, now a vessel of departure, bobbed against the shore. Ruby cast one last look at the island, its beauty now tinged with the haunting memory of loss. Andry, still grappling with the weight of grief, aided Ruby onto the boat.

As the shoreline gradually receded, Nosy Mangabe stood as a testament to the unpredictable dance between allure and peril, a stark reminder that not all treasures are worth such a great cost.

CHAPTER 5

Back at the airport, Ruby found herself adrift in a sea of contemplation.

The weight of her journal, tucked away in her bag, determined not to open the journal again for a long time, if ever. She bid farewell to Andry; silence enveloped them.

The guilt pressed against her shoulders, threatening to crush her under its weight.

The only solace she looked for was the comforting embrace of her pug, Gizmo, awaiting her at home—a haven where the tendrils of this harrowing experience could be gently unraveled and set aside.

That night, Ruby found herself jolted awake by a nightmare that lingered in the shadowy recesses of her subconscious. The panther's amber eyes, a vivid specter haunting her dreams, were poised to pounce. She awoke in a cold sweat, the imaginary teeth, and sharp claws of the panther hovering on the precipice of reality. The whole ordeal left her shaken, a residual echo of the trip.

The following morning, the domestic tranquility of Ruby's life was disrupted by the vibrant presence of her sister, Diamond. Clad in the sparkles that mirrored her namesake, Diamond was a radiant force, brimming with excitement to hear the tales of Ruby's island expedition. Ruby, still grappling with the emotional aftermath, welcomed the distraction as Gizmo energetically joined the morning reunion.

Ruby's twin sister, though sharing a striking resemblance, owned eyes of a mesmerizing grayish-white hue and hair that matched the pristine color. As Diamond animatedly recounted her own expedition to India at the age of 20, the mysterious nature of their family's birthright became clear. The journal, an heirloom passed down through generations, held secrets that were both a larger than she had first thought.

Warming up to Gizmo's affectionate licks and tummy rubs, Ruby spoke, "Hey, you startled me. I was so tired last night I didn't have the energy to talk to anyone. I just needed to sleep. How were things while I was gone?"

Gizmo, the loyal companion, wagged his tail hearing his name, his presence offering a comforting anchor amid the storm of emotions for Ruby.

Diamond teased, "Oh, just fine, right Gizmo? Yes, we spoiled you didn't we? Yes, we did!"

Observing Gizmo's slightly fuller figure, Ruby remarked, "I see that; he looks like he's put on a few pounds."

With a mischievous glint in her eyes, Diamond inquired about Ruby's journey, "So, how was your trip? Are you wiser and complete now?" Ruby, still grappling with the shadows of Nosy Mangabe, couldn't find solace in the narrative she had to share.

"Wiser? Um, but I didn't have a good time there. I didn't find it, and the trip was stopped suddenly due to an emergency the guide had," Ruby admitted, the weight of unfulfilled expectations etched across her face.

Diamond, surprised by the turn of events, exclaimed, "What? Why didn't you get another guide, then, silly? You went such a long way for nothing. That really sucks! How will you get your gem now?"

With a heavy sigh, Ruby explained, "Diamond, is it that important? I mean, it's just a stone. I didn't think of getting another guide. Besides, I was tired and just wanted to go home. The jungle is no place for a lady like me."

Diamond's eyes widened with disbelief, "Ruby? Is it just a stone? It's only the thing that brings us to our full potential. Don't you want to be whole?"

"I am whole as I am. Besides daddy has lots of money anyway, he will help me until I decide what I want to do. Like he said, I can work at the law firm, and I agreed to it, so I will be set," Ruby asserted, oblivious to the profound significance of the family's birthright.

Diamond, realizing a crucial omission in her past explanations, took a deep breath and said, "Okay, maybe no one has explained things to you, and that is my fault. After Mom died, I was more concerned about burying the past and getting on with our lives that I didn't stop to tell you how important that stone is to not only you but to our whole family. It makes us all stronger, not just you. It keeps the tradition, too."

The revelation hung in the air, a watershed moment that threatened to unravel the tapestry of Ruby's understanding. The family's birthright, once perceived as a mere trinket, now stood as a tether connecting generations, an embodiment of strength and tradition. As the weight of this newfound knowledge settled on Ruby, the realization dawned that her journey had only just begun—a journey to reclaim not just a stone, but the essence of her familial legacy.

CHAPTER 6

Ruby's eyes, laden with defiance, met Diamond's earnest gaze. "Well, I am the one who will be traveling and will decide if and when I need to go. I am in charge of my own destiny; the world won't end if I don't go, right? I have already decided, so please don't give me a lecture about it. When I am ready, I will go."

Diamond's expression shifted, a blend of concern and frustration etched on her features. "Ruby, time is not something you have the luxury of having. You need to get that gem sooner rather than later. It's a matter of principle, and it's your duty to this family. Besides that, I am not even sure if anyone has ever gotten the gems before. I don't know what kind of effect you could be causing our family by not having it in your possession."

Ruby let out an exasperated sigh, the weight of her sister's words pressing on her like an unwelcome burden. "Oh, come on, just because we have unique eyes, and our names are from gems doesn't mean we have to have them by our side. I mean, we turn 20 before we even get the journals. And who started this tradition anyway? Why is it so important? Is it to keep the wealth for the family? Pfft, please, I think I can work and not worry about a gem for a while. It's not going to affect anything, Diamond. I think, as usual, you are overreacting."

Diamond rose from the bed, her eyes pleading with Ruby to grasp the gravity of their legacy. "So, you don't even want to hear about it and understand why it's important? And it's not just about keeping the family wealthy. It could affect our health as a whole. I don't know exactly what since this has never happened before."

"NO, I don't want to know. Just leave it be, Diamond, please. I've had enough of this nonsense. I just want a normal life a job and some happiness."

The tension in the room lingered as Diamond, disheartened by Ruby's resistance, left the house without another word. The door closed with a muted finality, leaving behind a silence with unspoken truths. The emotional chasm between the sisters widened, each grappling with their own interpretation of what it meant to carry the weight of family expectations.

As Ruby remained alone in the room, the echo of their heated exchange reverberated within her. The conflict between tradition and personal autonomy tugged at the edges of her consciousness. The temptation of a conventional life, unburdened by the enigmatic duty tied to a gem, seemed increasingly appealing.

Yet, a gnawing uncertainty lingered, a subtle reminder that the tapestry of their family's history held threads of mystery and obligation.

Days passed, and the once vibrant camaraderie between Ruby and Diamond waned into an uneasy silence. The topic of the family gem became an unspoken taboo, a delicate fissure threatening to fracture their bond. Ruby, grappling with a sense of rebellion against the perceived shackles of tradition, immersed herself in the routine of an ordinary life.

One evening, as the sun dipped below the horizon, casting a warm glow across the room, Diamond cautiously approached Ruby. The air was charged with unspoken words, and Diamond, driven by a deep-seated concern, sought a bridge over the emotional divide.

"Ruby, can we talk?" Diamond's voice, tinged with a vulnerability that mirrored the setting sun, held a plea for understanding.

Ruby, pausing in her activities, met Diamond's gaze, her defenses momentarily softened. "Fine, talk."

Diamond took a deep breath, choosing her words with a delicate precision. "I know you want a normal life, Ruby, and I respect that. But this isn't about tradition or wealth. It's about something deeper, something that binds us as a family. I don't want to force you into anything, but I want you to consider the implications of turning away from our heritage. It's not just your burden; it's ours, collectively."

Ruby looked at the emotional plea in Diamond's eyes, sighing in response, "Alright, go ahead, enlighten me."

Diamond, seizing the opportunity to bridge the emotional gap, began unraveling the intricate layers of their family's history. The tale unfolded, weaving together threads of mystery, duty, and the delicate balance between individual aspirations and the collective destiny of their lineage. As the narrative unfolded, Ruby found herself drawn by their heritage.

Ruby, once adamant in her dismissal of tradition, began to glimpse the profound inter-connectedness that transcended individual desires.

In the days that followed, a subtle shift occurred within Ruby. The once-avoided topic of the family gem transformed into a dialogue that bridged the emotional tension between them.

Ruby still not convinced of the seriousness of finding her gem, did not venture back to Nosy Manabe.

CHAPTER 7

A year had passed, and Ruby was making great strides at the law firm. She managed in a year to make partner and had won so many cases that the firm had become a well-known company dealing with larger clientele.

Daddy retired from the firm and felt Ruby would be good to take over at some point but only when Ruby felt she was ready to take that on.

Ruby went jogging every morning with Gizmo, came home to have a shower, and had some coffee while she caught up on her social media before work.

She sat down and scrolled through Facebook. Diamond moved out after the long conversation about the gem. Now online was the only time she could see anything going on with her sister as she scrolled through her profile.

Ruby thought about that journal in a box in her closet that she hadn't touched since the trip.

Diamond missed her sister, and sure her sister was thinking about her at that same moment but knew it would have to be Ruby who wanted to talk now, nothing left for her to do or say at this point.

But Ruby was not about to get talked into going to look for that stone. Their thoughts intermingled with each other briefly.

On the other side of town where Ruby and her family lived, a science lab was investigating the fluctuation in power lately. Like something or someone was draining the city's energies. Derek Fieldman the head of the Science Department for Research on Exceptional Environmental Services of California was watching the area for energy surges.

Derek was a dirty blond mullet hairstyle loner with blue eyes. He had no girlfriend or hardly any friends at all. He was consumed with work. He wore those khaki style pants with pockets on the side. He had them in every color. He had a tribal bicep tattoo which he got when he was in shape back then but now made him look like a stereotypical meathead.

He heard an urban legend that there were people who were not exactly human living amongst them. They had a high content of mineral or precious gems in them that somehow created and protected the areas in which they lived, and he heard could potentially self-heal and travel by transformation into a sort of cloud matter.

But no one had ever seen it or was alive to verify it at least. To imagine that someone or something had control over the weather and the natural disasters in an area was fascinating.

Derek wanted to find out more and spoke to various people who heard the stories. He was told families were living in all parts of the world and they helped to keep the lands from droughts, hurricanes, and many other natural disasters. Their power covered a 1000-mile radius from the areas in which they lived.

It did sound crazy, but he was a scientist, so he wanted proof of this existence and wanted to harness its powers. The potential it could give someone to have that kind of control over an area could be monumental. Why they could charge money and make people pay them to keep them safe or take them to other places to stop one from potentially killing thousands of people.

In the office, Derek was not sure how that would work since he was finding that the opposite was happening now reading his graphs and the data, he collected over the past year seemed the exact opposite.

Last week, an earthquake rocked California which was on the scale of 3.5. It is significant for the area. They hadn't had any for 50 years so why now?

It was just an urban legend, Derek thought. "Mark, have you seen the latest stat readings for the prediction of our next earthquake? I want you to report any irregularities to me at once, understood?"

Mark was eating his morning donut, Yeah, he mumbled with crumbs falling from his mouth. Mark was Derek's assistant, and although much better looking and taller than Derek, who was heavy in the middle and always had a sour expression Mark knew no funny business when it came to him.

He had tried to tell jokes to break the ice and befriend him to no avail. "Hey what do you get when you cross an alien with a theoretical question?"
Derek just gave him an obvious shut-up stare and that was it. Mark knew when to bail out.

"Derek, I did have an email from another scientist from I.D.E.E.S (India Department of Exceptional Environmental Sciences) as you requested to inquire about that family living in India. They heard of this urban legend you had mentioned and are requesting more information on it as they would like to collaborate with you. I will send it to you now. I'm glad that we put out that mass email. We are already getting feedback."

"Interesting. Thank you."

Derek sat at his computer waiting for the email. Attached was data on the areas where they believed the 'exceptional family' was living. He rubbed his eyes and went over the data twice.

"Unbelievable." He muttered out loud.

CHAPTER 9

Ruby got home later than usual, having a hard time concentrating in the office and on paperwork which seemed to take forever to finish. Her mind kept wandering today and that was unusual for her, but she brushed it off to not enough coffee and late nights poring over files.

Gizmo greeted her at the door while twirling around in circles and accidentally peed in the entrance of the doorway which Ruby managed to step in again. Gizmo was getting older, and his bladder wasn't what it used to be. She thought about taking him to the vet.

She let him out and looked out at the night sky.

'It's never dark enough to see the stars well here,' she thought to herself. After dinner and a movie, she couldn't keep her eyes open she was just plain exhausted. It hadn't hit her this hard since he was on the island cutting that grass and sweating in the blazing sun.

Funny that was twice she thought about her trip today, she hadn't thought of it since she came home. She went to sleep instantly.

Sometime in the night she woke covered in sweat and gasping for air. She turned on the light and without thinking went to the box in her closet and got the journal.

Something wasn't right and she couldn't put her finger on it, but she had dreamt about the island and being in the heat, it felt so real like she was back there. She didn't open the journal just then she still couldn't bring herself to do it. She placed it on her night table and went back to sleep.

The next morning, she didn't go for a jog, she felt tired and didn't have the energy to. She drank her coffee and watched the news. News anchor, "Another natural disaster this morning, the heat in California was going up this summer and the forest fires were taking large chunks of land and people's homes. Please, be cautious, when out for long periods, drink plenty of water and try to stay indoors as much as possible."

Ruby didn't want to work today her energy was so low; she thought she was coming down with something. She called in and told them to rebook her appointments for tomorrow or have her partner cover them.

Daddy told her later he didn't have the energy he once had he felt weaker than usual and tired all the time over the phone. So, Ruby decided to pop in for a visit and see how he was doing.

"Hi Dad, how are you doing?" He let her in without as much as a word.

She turned to him and saw how much he had aged, recently. "Daddy are you okay? You don't seem your chipper self. I've taken the day off felt a little run down myself."

"I think I am just getting old is all," he coughed for the next couple of minutes that concerned her.

"Dad, did you get a journal when you turned 20 to find your stone?" I never really asked you about it and you never really talked much about it."

"No, that was your mother's side of the family tradition. You were blessed with that and now that you have the stone you will have so many wonderful things happen to you. "

"Daddy, I never actually got the gem when I went. I didn't tell you, but I didn't think it was a big deal. Diamond was going on about how important it was, and I told her to stop being over-dramatic about it that it was just a stone, and I will get it when I see fit." Ruby yawned, not being able to shake this tired feeling.

"Ruby, it is very important. That gem is a part of you. I don't know how to explain it without sounding strange but please listen to me. Your mother had a gift; she was born into a family whose blood ran with the gems of the names they were born into. That is the reason you are named Ruby you own this as well. That stone gives you strength it gives your sister strength and every descendant who is alive you are all connected in this way. In turn with this power, you can heal the earth from natural disasters and many other things which I am not sure only you who possess this stone can come into that power and be able to discover it." He looked at her with his kind brown eyes.

Ruby felt sick, she was affecting everyone around her by not getting the stone when she was meant to. The thought of making other people ill or in danger made her feel terrible. Especially her sister Diamond, she didn't want anything to happen to her.

"I had no idea. Dad, I am so sorry. Why didn't you tell me this before? Shouldn't I have the right to know before now?" Ruby was frustrated with him; it was his responsibility to tell her who she was.

"After your mom died, I did the best I could, I wanted you to have a normal life like all the other children so I let it be, I was hoping you would come to understand when you read the journal and got the stone. I was not aware you didn't have it in your possession.

"Now, I fear that this might be the cause of some of the things going on in California. You have to find a way to retrieve that stone. I would go with you, but I think it would be too much for me to manage. Your sister can?" He looked down at his mug.

"Okay dad I will figure it out, I am sorry for jumping down your throat just now. I know you did your best and I love you, dearly." Ruby leaned over and kissed him on the forehead before walking out to find her sister.

CHAPTER 10

Derek got off the phone with the scientist in China they also heard about it and was interested in obtaining information on what to look for when trying to obtain a gauge on if any families were living in the area.

He knew he was on to something now, but he needed a device that could pinpoint the exact location of the family in question.

"What is the status on the power surge readers do we have any updates? I needed that yesterday and now with more people inquiring about it we have to get on this before anyone else so we can be the leader in the search. I believe we will be able to find them quickly since we already know the town in which the changes have been taking place."

"I was talking with our head engineer, and he believes he has one ready to be evaluated in the next few days. However, he can only produce the one until he can obtain more parts from the companies who manufacture it." Mark talked to him while hovering over his laptop.

"Good, I will be taking a road trip over to those areas immediately; something has to be done about the environmental effects of this phenomenon!" His voice was sounding desperate, small, and lost.

It hadn't rained in weeks and the fires were taking over, news of earthquakes was becoming more and more frequent. The temperatures soared as the sun burned down and was relentless. Day in and day out the news had more and more disasters now spreading all over the world. Something was indeed happening, and Derek was determined to find out exactly the cause of all this and put a stop to it once and for all.

CHAPTER 11

Ruby couldn't find her sister; she wasn't at work and not at home. She called her cell half a dozen times, checked Facebook, and still had no clue.

She decided to go home, "I am sure she will show up at some point," she muttered to herself.

It was hot as hell out and she was tired, she always felt tired lately. Her energy was depleted, and it was not getting any better.

After supper, she sat on her bed to go to bed early. She looked at her nightstand and saw the journal sitting where she left it.

She picked it up and decided to read it.

August 3, 1976

Our journey into the caves of Madagascar proved to be in vain today spent the day searching for the jewel but to no avail. I have been here for more than a week and I am desperate to find it and go back to my life as I knew it.

Andry has been very kind to me but tells me that I need to search for it with my heart. I don't know what that means. I am tired now but will try again in the morning. I believe that I will come across it if I am diligent.

August 4, 1976

I went to a new part of the cave today which I passed by every day and never noticed before. On the cave wall was inscribed a message from past tribal people who wrote on the walls in symbols. I wish I knew what they meant. But the drawings looked to show the woman being gifted with a gem. She was shining this light all over the town and the town's people are bowing and giving her gifts.

Perhaps if I go further into that part of the cave, I will be able to find it. I am hopeful. Andry is such a lovely man. I have grown quite fond of him. He has so many stories of the land and tales of a woman like in the cave that helps the town from natural disasters.

I laughed but he was serious, said it was something they believed in for centuries and it was tradition to help those who would be empowered with the gem. I am starting to think that there is a connection between what I am looking for and the stories they told. But I cannot imagine my inheritance being anything more than a stone that keeps wealth in our family.

Hopefully, tomorrow, we will find it.

Ruby read the pages with great fascination; the gem had no significance to environmental factors? That is just crazy. She yawned and fell asleep, her eyes heavy from reading and lack of energy.

The next morning, she woke to her phone ringing, "Hello?" She was barely awake.

"Hi, it's me. My coworker said you were looking for me. Fine time to go looking for me now when I am out of town on vacation." Diamond said in a quiet voice.

She was still not happy with her sister for not letting her explain things and how they left the last conversation. They hadn't spoken in so long, but it felt like yesterday. They used to be so close; they did everything together as kids. They even believed they could read each other's thoughts. They exchanged clothes and had the same mutual friends. Joined at the hip some people would say.

"Oh, where are you? And your work never mentioned you were on vacation. I wanted to apologize for my behavior in our last conversation. It was not like me to ignore advice from you but under the circumstances, I was in no position to discuss it. If you have a minute I would like to explain." Ruby sat up in her bed and looked at the journal.

"Sure, I appreciate you saying that as I was pretty mad at you, well up until now still was." Diamond's tone was softer now.

"I figured that. Well, the short story of what happened was the guide who took me to find the gem his son was killed in a terrible accident involving a panther. They protected me and I was in shock, and I felt like it was my fault that it happened because if I hadn't been there looking for that stupid jewel, he might still be alive." Ruby's voice broke up with the last sentence.

"Oh Ruby, I am so sorry, I wish you would have told me this sooner! How awful. But you must understand something important, and I need you to just listen. It's going to sound crazy at first, but you must be feeling it by now so perhaps you will get what I am trying to say."

"The gem is connected to all of us, it keeps us in our strength, and it helps us help the world too. So, in having it with us we are strong not just as an individual but as a family. And at twenty that is the time when you are old enough to become one with the powers of the jewel you have pulsing in your blood. I don't know how you are feeling but it is affecting me personally, I feel drained lately and daddy said that aunty Safire has been ill as of late too.

"We need to get that jewel into your hands now the time is flying by, and things are happening that I think if I explained anymore, you would think I am nuts. Just please believe me when I tell you that we need that jewel for everyone, not just you or our family."

Ruby felt a wave of fear come over her; she knew she needed to get that gem.

CHAPTER 12

In a quaint Chinese town, an elderly woman named Sue grappled with the inexorable pull and depletion of advancing years. Gazing at the blue topaz gem embedded in her bicep, she saw its intermittent flickering within the rays of light it emitted.

A disconcerting realization dawned on Sue – something was amiss. Her husband, Li, had recently met a mysterious demise that confounded medical explanations, leaving her world shattered. While life itself remained uncertain, she found solace in the knowledge that Li had not endured undue suffering. Their union, devoid of offspring, had been an anchor in her existence. Their fateful encounter, marked by the exchange of glances revealing the gems in their eyes, kindled a love that endured. Yet only those sharing their unique nature could discern the gems; to others, her eyes appeared ordinary.

The silver-haired fair complexion Sue, a fixture in the local street markets, peddled fruits to the valley residents. For years, Li had sourced the produce from a neighboring town at a discounted rate, ensuring a profitable venture. However, with his passing, Sue faced the daunting task of charting a new course for survival.

Such anomalies were unheard of in her family, known for their longevity and robust health. The gem, a guardian of sorts, traditionally safeguarded the village from calamities. Yet, the recent events unfolded in the community hinted it was diminishing. Sue, despite her longevity, found herself unable to shield the village from these unprecedented new adversities.

A mere week prior, a devastating mudslide wreaked havoc, claiming hundreds of houses and the lives of cherished friends in the dead of night.

As Sue grappled with concerns about her home's precarious location near the town's edge and the adjacent river, she contemplated the uncertain future. The waning strength of the gem, once a formidable protector, now raised fears of impending calamities.

"What is happening to me?" she muttered and looked on at the devastation the mudslide had caused.

CHAPTER 13

Derek, after receiving the much-anticipated approval for the conceptual Power Reader Informatory, abbreviated as CPI, a sleek and compact pocket device. It proved to be not only convenient for portability but also slated for imminent availability to fellow scientists eager to explore the enigmatic phenomenon.

Engaged in online operations, Derek gradually noticed the device coming to life as he unconsciously steered his vehicle toward the direction where Ruby and her father lived. This innovative reader had the capability to meticulously track fluctuations in core power surges on a grand scale, presenting the data in a visually intuitive bar graph that ranged from low to high. Additionally, it boasted a feature supplying the map a location of the detected area, pinpointing two distinct locations.

Despite the abundance of such occurrences on a global scale, the device lacked the in-depth information needed. To fill this gap, a more substantial apparatus was in the works at their office. Derek accelerated towards his destination, propelled by the urgency of the moment. However, the signal strength appeared feeble, prompting him to tap the side of the device, ensuring the accuracy of the readings it presented.

As Derek pulled up to the beginning of the street, a surge of excitement echoed in his pounding heart. He whispered to himself, "This is it; finally, I will obtain the answers I seek. If my suspicions are correct, I will join the ranks of the foremost scientists unraveling the mysteries of this extraordinary power." Speaking aloud, he disembarked from his antiquated 1999 Oldsmobile Buick, ready to embark on this transformative journey.

CHAPTER 14

Feeling a surge of anxiety during the conversation, Ruby interjected, cutting Diamond off before she could continue, "Where are you right now? I'll come to you. We need to retrieve this gem, and I could use your help. Will you join me? You never really talked about how you acquired your gem during your twentieth birthday expedition."

"I'm currently in New York, visiting a friend's cottage. I'm about to head to the airport. Why don't you meet me in Madagascar? I'll catch a flight out today instead of returning home, and we can embark on this journey together. I'll explain everything when we meet, alright?" Diamond's location was clear from the background noise of honking horns and bustling activity in New York.

Without hesitation, Ruby expressed her gratitude, "I'll pack my bag now and go. Thank you for coming with me, sis." The prospect of revisiting that place unnerved her, especially after what had transpired.

"That's what family is for. Plus, I've missed my best friend. I can't wait to see you. We'll retrieve the gem, and everything will be better, you'll see. I love you."

"I love you too, Diamond." Ruby ended the call, swiftly grabbed her travel bag, and began packing. Gizmo wagged his tail and sniffed curiously investigating her belongings on the bed.

"I'll have to drop you off at Papa's, my little cutie."

Without wasting any time, Ruby exited out the door, speeding down the road in her sleek black BMW, barely pausing at the stop sign as she unknowingly passed by Derek.

CHAPTER 15

Derek, briskly walking toward the house, was abruptly jolted by a sudden surge in readings as Ruby sped away in her car.

"What the...?" He squinted at the Power Reader Informatory (CPI), checking the map that showed the device had just passed him. Reacting swiftly, he ran back to his car, determined to pursue whatever had triggered such an anomaly. Engrossed in examining the CPI, Derek collided with a neighbor who was jogging, resulting in a chaotic tumble. The impact shattered his precious reader into a thousand pieces.

"What the hell, man? Why don't you look where you're going?" The twenty-something neighbor, adorned with glistening sweaty muscles and tanned thighs, rose from the ground, inspecting the damage done to his temple-like physique.

Derek seethed, "Me? Look what you've done, you idiot! You've destroyed a valuable piece of government property. You should be the one to be sorry!"

"Whatever, man. Clearly, you ran into me, staring at that thing like you were about to kiss it." Without waiting for more words, the young man resumed his jog, putting distance between himself and Derek.

Derek's face contorted with anger, transforming into a pained expression. Limping from a scraped knee sustained during the collision, he retrieved his cell phone, the frustration clear in his actions. As the phone rang, he felt as though he had walked into a wall, considering the guy he collided with was built like a brick house. Rubbing his injured knee, Derek answered the phone.

"Mark, we have a problem. I've broken the device. I don't want to get into it right now, just get them to make me another one so I have it tomorrow morning. I am taking the rest of the day off." He didn't wait for Mark's reply, swiftly hanging up before any response could be given.

CHAPTER 16

Ruby dropped Gizmo off at her dad's, she noticed how weak he was, and the dog looked so very tired too. Ruby said she would be back as soon as she could. She didn't have time to explain.

At the airport, she bought her ticket and waited patiently for her flight.

"Hey is this seat taken?" Gentlemen dressed in a well-made tailored business suits approached Ruby while she read more of the journal logs from her Aunt.

"No, no you can sit it's no problem no one is sitting here. She noticed his eyes right away and how striking they were. They looked hazel with beautiful gold flecks that seemed to sparkle as he spoke.

"Lucky for me then, my feet are killing me. I will be glad to be on my way. Sorry I am sure you don't want to hear my woes." He chuckled.

That's quite alright you just caught me off guard is all. I was engrossed in my reading, and you startled me." Ruby blushed from how hand-some he was.

"Name is Charlie, what's yours? You off to somewhere grand I imagine?"

"Well, I am meeting my sister in Madagas-car so it's not grand, but it is exotic I suppose." Ruby tried to compose herself as his facial features seem to draw her in and she was becoming increasingly warm.

"Ah, well that is exotic. I am going there myself but not for vacation for business. I have a few meetings there. So, we will be on the same flight then. I am feeling like this might be my best trip yet if I get to sit next to a lovely lady such as yourself." Charlie also felt warm, she was beautiful, and he'd been looking at her for ten minutes across the room before getting up the courage to talk to her.

"Well, I am flattered thank you. May I ask what field of business you are in?"

"Oh, you'd be bored in the details, but I will just say this I dabble in real estate and my boss has me looking for a vacation home for him on one of the islands there." Charlie fidgeted with his tie as he spoke.

"I see, well I work for a law firm so, lots of yawning there in my field too. What island is it he was thinking of?" Ruby's curiosity got the better of her. Hoping it was the same island but what would the odds of that be?

"Ah, I doubt being a lawyer is boring. Um, you know I think there was more than one, to be honest. I have to find the best three and email him the details so he can decide. It doesn't hurt that it is nice places so I will enjoy looking for them." Charlie smiled his best smile, the one that melted women's hearts.

"Nice," she smiled back, and her heart skipped a beat.

CHAPTER 17

A man from Jamaica named Emerald clutched his left bicep; the Emerald stone flickered on his arm. He was in his late forties and worked hard every day of his life. He had a large family of children, three girls, and two boys.

He owned a shop by the tourist area where he sold fresh fish and other items that were supplied for his family. But lately, his energy was quite low. He had trouble staying awake and fishing out in the sea. He looked at his arm and noticed a rash was developing from the gem to his hands. It was a deep red and blisters were forming. He had been having trouble breathing today and felt the oxygen was not getting to his brain fast enough. He staggered home and sat on the couch; his children played around him and didn't notice him but his youngest.

"Daddy are you okay? You look like you are sick? Are you sick?"

"I, ya, daddy is not feeling well today. Fetch me some water please maybe I just need a drink." The young girl named Alisha went to get it.

When she returned, he was sleeping on the couch, she placed it beside him on the coffee table and went to go play with her siblings.

CHAPTER 18

On the plane Ruby and Charlie got to know each other, they talked about everything and anything. She confided in him that she was going there to look for something of her birthright and didn't want to go because of the incident that took place when she was there last. She felt she could trust him he was a mind-spirit and she read his thoughts through his eyes easily.

Charlie took her hand in his, "I know that I haven't known you long but if there is anything I can do to help you I would gladly do it for you."

Ruby for the second time blushed, his hand was so warm and inviting. He was gentle with her. She was taken with him and wanted him to come with her on the trip to find the gem.

"Thank you, for that, I am flattered you would want to, but I can't put you out you have work but maybe we can meet up if all goes well with both of us."

"I would be happy to see you again I don't want this flight to end if I am honest. You are a beautiful and interesting woman, and I would love to get to know you better." He kissed her hand and looked into her eyes. Ruby's eyes twinkled brightly as she smiled at him and gave him her number.

CHAPTER 19

Derek walked in the next morning with a large band-aid around his knee. He had a fresh coffee in hand and was ready for business as he went to Mark's desk for the device.

"Hi there, what happened to your knee? Jeez, you weren't kidding must have been some kind of accident. I got a joke that might cheer you up." Mark eyeballed Derek's knee so much, it was making him feel uncomfortable.

"It's nothing, listen I need another new reader now. I have to go back out there and see if I can find that surge again. And, no, I don't want to hear your extremely cheesy jokes Mark they aren't funny."

"Well," said Mark with a twinkle of mischief in his eye. "I have something even better that just got approved. Follow me."

In the far corridor of the large scientific operation was a grey box with dozens of tiny lights which was the first thing Derek noticed. Upon turning the corner, he looked up at the wall, saw a map of the earth, and noticed glowing entities from all over covering one end of the globe to another. In amongst it was one that was floating on water as it slowly moved to what looked like an African area.

"Shit! They did it!"

He couldn't believe his eyes. They took the device and specs that were in the prototype and turned it into a global scale reader.

"Yup, they've been working on it in conjunction with the small-scale scanner you had sent specs to and turned it into what you see before you. It's pretty amazing. I didn't think this was real, to be honest with you, but now that I see for myself, I am a believer. So, all those dots are people who have some kind of power?"

Mark scratched his head. He was just Derek's assistant, not a scientist.

"Well, that is the theory and I have to prove it and figure out how to harness it for the greater good."

Derek was still staring at the screen on the wall.

CHAPTER 20

Diamond ran up to Ruby and hugged her tight, "Are you ready for this? I called ahead and got Andry to meet us. He was so sorry for the way things went. They are better prepared for us now he said. Do not need to worry. I am so excited to do this with you."

"Right" She looked off at the direction of where Charlie had left her just minutes before.

"Everything okay?"

"Yeah, I'm just a little distracted."

"Ah yes, the tall dark, and handsome man you met on the plane." Diamond giggled.

"Hey now stop reading my thoughts you." She smiled.

The trip was longer than before but finally, they were back on the Island of Nosy Mangabe. Both of them looked dusty and exhausted and Andry could sense that they had enough and set up camp for them along with a larger team of 8 men, some of which carried shotguns and others camping gear and other supplies.

Andry looked as if he had aged since the last time, she had seen him. They all sat by the fire ate a beautiful meal once again and enjoyed the crackling fire. It was mesmerizing, they talked very little. Diamond went to bed and Ruby followed shortly after. Both were not up for being social, sleep was more important.

The next morning Ruby awoke to the smell of fresh coffee brewing. Sun was shining and the sky was a beautiful tropical turquoise blue.

"Morning Andry, it's a beautiful day out." Ruby grabbed herself a coffee and sat beside him.

"Yes, it is beautiful today; I hope that we have some success in getting that gem for you. Have you been reading your aunt's journal? I hope that she left some clues for you to make it easier. But nothing compares to feeling it with your heart to find something you're connected to understand?"

"I think I do yes, I've been reading it and am starting to see that it's more about connection then an object to find." Ruby sipped on her

coffee. "You are right sis, and once you understand that you are finding a piece of yourself you
will be more aware of its presence." Diamond
grabbed herself a cup of coffee and sat next to
Ruby.

"I know I am in good company so I can
show you something now which I didn't think you
would understand before."

Diamond put her coffee down beside her
and tried to lift her sleeve to reveal the diamond
placed in her left bicep. It was inserted inside her
skin, but the flat side of the jewel protruded ever
so slightly. It was flickering which looked as
though there was a light behind it.

Ruby gasped and without thought reached
out to gently touch it. It was about three inches
wide and two inches long. Without words, Ruby
lifted her biceps and looked to see if there were
marks on her skin where hers would be.

Nothing.

"Listen, the gem is a part of you, and we
have gifted the right to protect the world with the
Earth's most precious gifts. We are not like ordinary people; we are from an ancient descendent

of people who believed in heating the gems melting them down and drinking them.

"And for centuries the children born from the parents drank it formed us, and it continues to this day. Your children will be special too if you choose to have any. Because of this we also have the power to hurt but it is a choice to care for those who cannot help us. It is up to you to decide how you wish to deal with your gifts."

Diamond looked at her sister with love in her eyes.

"Because you choose not to get the gem when it was time for you too, unfortunately, it has had dire consequences. The world is in chaos and some people are feeling the effects of your choices including me."
Diamond lifted her sleeve more and revealed a deep dark redness in her shoulder, it looked to be infected.

"Oh my god! What have I done? I have been so selfish, and I am hurting you. I am so sorry." Ruby hugged her sister and for the first time in a long time cried hard.

"Shh, it's okay. Part of this is that we cannot choose things for other people, and you had to learn in your own time. But the time is now to set things right, but only if you truly want to." Diamond picked up her coffee mug and looked over at Andry.

"Miss, you must open your heart and have a love for others and this world and that is the only way to be, but it is up to you, we are all connected to nature and each other."

Andry was packing up things while he spoke. He turned away from her now and wiped his eyes. He had been crying too for the pain of losing his son, it was still very fresh in his mind.

CHAPTER 21

Derek saw with a mix of excitement and trepidation as the energy in Madagascar appeared to halt, a stark contrast to its movement beforehand. Its brilliance had surpassed all the other energies he had met.

"Mark, what is the number for the scientific environment headquarters in Madagascar?"

"One sec I will send that via text for you."

Mark was stuffing another donut into his face, so it was a muffled response with bits of donut falling onto his keyboard. Derek called and spoke to a man named Paul who had been in the chain letters of emails from India, China, and Jamaica, sent as mass mail to get feedback on any irregularities in energies in the area and natural disasters that could not be explained.

"We've detected strong energy here off the island, similar to readings from about a year ago. We're sending investigators to pinpoint its exact location. Any updates on your end?" Paul's accent made it challenging for Derek to grasp every word.

"No, it vanished into thin air. I lost track of it when... Anyway, I'd be very interested in your findings. If it's someone or something, please set up a perimeter and don't let it leave. I'll come down to take over and oversee the results," Derek conveyed, determined to be at the forefront of this discovery.

As he conversed with Paul, Derek simultaneously booked a flight using his app, unwilling to let another scientist uncover the secrets of this colossal energy before he did.

"We'll keep you updated Derek, no problem. It should be easy now that you sent us the tech to track it as of last week," assured Paul.

Derek ended the call, his frustration clear. "Who issued the tech to go out before I approved it, Mark?" His face turned red with anger.

"It is in the government's hands now, and they were very interested in this project, so it went above pay grade and went out without any of us knowing until you mentioned it just now." Mark bit his thumbnail, he knew about it, but he was told to keep quiet about it.

"Well, I will be taking a few days off I have a long overdue vacation in order, since it's out of my hands," Derek confirmed his flight for tonight on his phone and started to gather some data and info needed to track the energies.

"Oh... okay. That's odd to leave now isn't it? We are right in the middle of a breakthrough, and you want to leave? You sure you want to go now? I mean, what if something important happens, how will I reach you?" Mark was pretending to be concerned but glad for some time away from him.

"It's called a cellphone, Mark, and I am sure the big wigs who took over my project can manage it just fine. Clearly they don't need my help anymore." With that, he walked out of the building, slamming the door behind him, leaving a trail of tension in the air.

CHAPTER 22

Off the coast of Ireland, Connemara stood looking out onto the water from the sandy fringes of the island's green shades off the shore. She was only nineteen and yet had the distinct feeling she was going to be stuck on this island forever.

She was young with beautiful green eyes like the marble she was named after. She was a savage beauty and all those around her said she was the pride of the island. She would do great things her papa said when she was little. Her parents carefully crafted her into the person they thought she should be giving her music lessons and teaching her ballet to be an elegant lady of society.

Yet, as she looked out to the sea her heart longed to visit other places and go on adventures. Lately, she had been feeling down on things and couldn't shake the feeling of being tired all the time. Her mama's recent passing didn't help matters and her heart was heavy with grief. She looked down at her hand and in it was the marble gifted to her early from her mother's death bed.

Her mother removed it from her arm just three passed just three days ago and told her to keep it close. She hugged it into her chest and slowly moved it to her left bicep; her tears flowed like a river. It was the same side as mama had when she removed it.

As if her body knew what to do it swallowed it and it then reappeared gently on her arm flickered and pulsed a soft green glow. She knew her life was now set just like the stone. She had to stay to protect the place she grew up in and this was her gift to the world but a curse for her.

Connemara walked back home when the sea turned calm and the sun returned shortly after, knowing she had to take care of papa because he needed her, they all did. But in its place, it caused a great sadness deep within her and deep depression from what is demanded of her. Its obligation and tradition of the way things were meant to be from the others before her and the thousands of years the weight of responsibility toward the heritage of her people.

CHAPTER 23

Ruby opened the journal and read another passage from her aunt Safire:

August 17, 1976.

Andry said I should close my eyes and just feel for where it is. I am too pig-headed to see *what is right in front of me. My pride is getting the better of me and I am worried I will never find it. I grow weary of this search and want to give up, but I know that I can't for people are counting on me, you reading this wouldn't be here if I didn't get what I came to be.*

So, I will continue for you future reader I know that I will have to dig deep within myself to open my heart and stop being so logical with things. I have trouble being kind and trusting and I have been selfish thinking that I am better than others. I have had to look at myself and see my ugly truths.

Tomorrow if I am lucky, I will find a part of me that is seeking me.

Ruby closed the journal and thought about who she was and how she felt about other people in her life and especially those she didn't know. She felt a connection to her aunt, they were simi-lar she always thought she was better for having money and for being in a good position in life ever since she was a child. She was arrogant in her thinking too.

"Miss, the cave is here just beyond those trees, it is well hidden, and I haven't been here since Safire." Andry looked at the cave with fond memories and a smile appeared on his face for the first time on this trip.

Diamond was just behind her and touched her shoulder, "Everything is going to be okay. Once you get the gem, we will be able to go back home and return to our lives as we know it."

"I will be happy about that! I am looking forward to shopping sprees, and lattes." Ruby giggled.

CHAPTER 24

Derek stepped off the plane and looked around. He stretched his arms out and smiled. "Here I come." People looked at him as he talked to himself with a devilish type grin.

He called ahead and got a man who could lead him to the middle of the island where the last pinpointed location of the energy was coming from.

It was a tourism agency that dealt with ex-peditions. "Best one on the island," the man said. "We would have another guide who would suit your needs better, but he is already on an expe-dition."

Within hours he was in the exact spot as Ruby and the others were just twelve hours ago. The man who was his guide carried a shotgun with a large backpack carrying everything needed. Two other men came along with guns and supplies.

CHAPTER 25

Andry and Diamond thought it best that Ruby go on her own and find the gem. They waited at the entrance.

Ruby entered the cave; it was cool damp and dark. She could hear water dripping in the distance. It had turns and twists as if at water ran through these walls as the rock was smooth to the touch and glistened when the light shone on it. She shone the light on the Journal and read the passage:

Deep within the passages of the cave, there appeared to be an arched doorway; she felt a tingle in her left arm. She closed her eyes and decided to follow her aunt's instructions. She scanned the walls with her hands and walked slowly; it was narrow enough to put both hands on either side.

Her heart started beating faster; she felt an indent in the wall and instinctively pressed it. A perfect circle that would otherwise be hidden opened up and revealed the jewel to her. It was lit up on its own and it pulsed with life at the same rhythm as her heart.

She didn't need her flashlight as its red rays of light filled the cave with it. She touched it and it felt remarkably warm. Carefully she picked it up and tears fell from her eyes. She could help her sister now and everything would be alright.

Without thought, she lifted her sleeve and went ahead to insert the ruby which her body welcomed it and her skin as if it were home en-gulfed it at once and it went into perfect place-ment. She felt a tingling rush throughout her body as she stood there in the very spot her aunt did so many years ago. Her mind started to see things and she knew things suddenly about her ancestors.

"Lapillus Populus," she muttered out loud.

As if she was in a trance, it was suddenly disrupted by screams outside. She could hear her sister calling for her and men were shouting. Ruby opened her eyes and started to run, just barely making out what her sister was saying, "Ruby run!"

She ran out of the cave just then and men all in camo with machine guns and full body armor were pointing guns at Andry his men and Diamond and had them surrounded. She ducked quickly behind the bushes. The men were on their walkie-talkies with their back to her, "We have the source, yes sir we have obtained the package. Ten-four we will get them to the lab in the mainland as soon as the chopper gets here. We are looking for one more, but we will find it, we have it surrounded."

Ruby panicked and decided to make a run for it.

CHAPTER 26

Unknowingly, Derek was shortly behind them and approaching the area fast. He was hot on her trail.

Ruby headed into the dense jungle, sweat pouring down her face as her hair stuck to her in the heat she couldn't think clearly. They had her sister it would only be a matter of time before they would catch her too. She looked up and saw two amber eyes glowing amongst the trees and her heart started beating fast.

She froze, heard the men breaking branches with their feet not far behind her. She leaned against the tree near some thick bamboo and didn't take her eyes off the panther as it stretched and slowly stood up deciding the best way to approach its meal.

The panther hopped to the tree its nails digging into the tree's trunk as it walked slowly.

She was leaning on the one across from him and he showed her its yellowish fangs, it was starting to come down the tree as the gun fired off in the distance. The sound was deafening. Derek pointed the gun at Ruby.

"Let's go, Nice and slow. Be quiet now I don't want them to hear us." He grabbed her by the arm tightly and pushed her violently forward in another direction away from the men. "Move, run now!" He barked. She looked at the panther that had stopped in his tracks from the gunfire and ran off high into the trees. Dinner would have to wait for another day.

Ruby ran as instructed not knowing who Derek was or where he came from. They ran until they couldn't hear the men anymore. Both exhausted, he sat down and pulled her down with him. It started to rain which muffled the noises in the jungle from hearing anything but the sound of it pelting down on the shiny wet leaves.

Derek began to talk with a stupid grin on his face, "I can't wait to show you to those government asses who stole my discovery. Yup, as long as I can get you out of here, they will be begging me to give you over to them. Then they will see who they were messing with." He laughed maniacally with a crazed look on his face

"So, what are you exactly?" Derek wiped his forehead as the sweat and rain mixed and fell into his eyes his smile was devilish and evil. Before Ruby could answer a bullet whizzed by her head and shot Derek in the head. He rolled to the jungle floor like a stone with his eyes still open. Ruby screamed. Diamond was in handcuffs and was being dragged by an officer about six feet tall and looked to weigh three times the size of both the sisters. His gun smoked as he pointed it at Ruby.

"Well for someone who has supposed powers you don't look like nothing much more than a weak woman. Let's go." The man said in a southern accent.

They walked the way they came and saw the remains of what the gunfire was about, Andry's men were all dead and scattered lying in the mud. The fresh blood was still oozing from their victim's wounds which had their distorted shocked faces frozen in time. Ruby looked to see if Andry was amongst them, she couldn't spot him, he got away.

The helicopter flew above, and a ladder rope was dropped down, Ruby, diamond and the men climbed in as it began its trip to the mainland. Ruby rubbed her arm and sat in silence; she was wet, sweaty, and covered in mud from the walk back. The men didn't speak to them and that at least was a comfort. The sky was unusually dark for this time of day as they flew above the water. The rain was continuing to pour down heavily and at such speed from the wind making it hard for the pilot to see and keep it a smooth ride.

Diamond was looking tired, dirty, and scared. Her sleeve was ripped, and it exposed the decay that had started on her arm. It didn't look any better yet and it concerned Ruby. The turbulence started to pick up as they held on to the railing; Ruby looked to her left and saw the hurricane funnel coming towards them.

"Whoa looks like we are in for a rough ride," the pilot tried to veer away from it sending the helicopter to turn on its side.

Ruby grabbed on for dear life and held her sister's hand. The helicopter spun out of control and was nose-diving for the water. The men had parachutes and jumped out without looking back leaving the two women in the helicopter.

Ruby looked at her sister, "Listen, we need to jump out of this helicopter right now do you hear me?"

Ruby was screaming over the noise from the machine and the whipping storm. It was so loud it was hard to hear anything else. Diamond nodded her head and tried to undo the seatbelt. It was jammed. Ruby saw her struggling with it and tried to help. They both yanked and pulled as hard as they could. The water was getting closer and the time to jump out was getting shorter.

CHAPTER 27

As Sue strolled to her shop, she sensed a noticeable shift within herself. Glancing discreetly at her arm, she saw that it was once again fully aglow. The collective energy of her fellow beings, bound by a shared ancestry and connection, had played its intended role in harmonizing. A reassuring smile formed on her face as she acknowledged that everything would now be alright somehow.

CHAPTER 28

Connemara sat on the plane. The captain said over the intercom that the temperature in Jamaica was a lovely sunny ninety-five Fahrenheit when they were to arrive.

She felt satisfied with herself. Everything she ever wanted was coming true an Adventure and travel just like she dreamed about.

Her father was angry to discover her sneaking out the window late last night with her backpack and begged her to stay. He needed her and the island needed her he pleaded but she was unmovable. She had already made up her mind.

She didn't care anymore, and she wanted to be free of her obligations, she didn't want the responsibility. She left the stone behind as she cut it out of her arm and decided to start a new life and that's when hell broke loose. Her rejecting her family's jewel had consequences just as Ruby had.

Bandaged up and sore she rubbed it and asked for some ice from the flight attendant.

CHAPTER 29

Ruby frantically pulled with all her might, in a few seconds they would be affected by the water and at the speed, it was going they would be crushed by the pressure. Diamond looked calmly at her sister. "You must save yourself. We don't have time and I cannot get free."

"NO, I won't leave you!" Ruby's eyes filled with tears as she struggled to find a way to get her free from the seat belt that was about to kill her sister. Her arms and hands became burning hot as she kept trying to pull on the seatbelt. She could feel something tingle from her left bicep to her hand as her frustration and anger grew.

The Helicopter plummeted into the depths of the sea and the aircraft began to take on water as it sank fast down into the tropical warm waters. Ruby's arm began to glow red and somehow she became increasingly strong and pulled Diamond easily from the seatbelt as it ripped apart as if made of paper.

Diamond on impact was hit in the head by the metal parts of the roof on impact and became unconscious. Ruby held on to her and on the other hand began to break herself free from the helicopter which was now more like a cement block tying them down as it was drifting deeper and deeper into the darkness of the sea.

After finding the weakness in the metal by feeling it with her hands she kicked it with both feet and it finally broke free. She at once swam to the surface and gasped for air as she came up. Her sister was still out cold and all she could do was keep her afloat and try to get her bearings as the winds started to die down enough for the swells to be manageable to be able to swim.

Ruby could see land off in the distance and swam as best she could while keeping her sister from taking on any more water. She cried out to her to wake up but the only sound to be heard was the wind from the remaining storm left from the hurricane that kept howling in her ears. Ruby's arms and hands remained glowing red and alt-hough she could still feel the strength in them she was exhausted. Ruby's eyes started to glow red now as she thought about losing her sister a deep feeling of loss overcame her and she was taken over by the rage of not knowing how to access this power she had.

"Dammit! How can I save you?!" she slapped the water with her free hand in frustration and then put both hands on her sister.

She closed her eyes and felt the love she had for her older sister. She couldn't imagine not having her in her life. She felt a tingle in her arms once more and Diamond began to moan softly, "Ruby what happened?"

"Thank god! You're awake!" she grasped onto her and held her tight. Hot tears flushed her eyes as she knew everything would be alright. "Diamond you have a head wound, you must try to relax, and I will get you to shore. Save your energy." Ruby looked at the deep gash on her forehead to the center of her head. It was dark and still bleeding.

"It's okay Ruby just watch." Diamond put her hand on her head and closed her eyes. The hands became a beacon of bright white and the surrounding waters began to light up from her entire body now fully glowing. Ruby swam back from her as she watched her sister heal herself. In a matter of minutes, Diamond's head was now pink and the gap in her head was closed to reveal a fresh pink line.

"Wow, that is remarkable. I felt as if I would not be able to save you. My hands did glow but not fully like that." Ruby was amazed and as they both floated in the water they looked to the land and knew that swimming for it would only be the beginning of the challenges they had ahead of them.

"We all have a unique set of talents. One of the common ones is the ability to heal ourselves. You will have to discover what yours are. You have healing elements in you too, but it must be learned. Let's get out of here and get dry first. But not all wounds heal especially the ones that are caused from ones like us." Diamond said as she started to swim for shore.

CHAPTER 30

The government had lost contact with the helicopter. The general named Frank Yeidman, who was in the secret service, took over overseeing the first project from Derek now had to deploy more men discretely to not raise any alarms to any surrounding local citizens. The monitor showed the energy had tripled in power and the glow on the screen was now large.

They were still alive, which meant they were vital in obtaining before they could figure out how to escape. Mark was not aware that Derek was dead, and although Frank gave the go-ahead to kill all witnesses in the vicinity, he was not about to jeopardize him knowing that information. It would be considered instead as classified which was above his pay grade anyway.

"We have a lock on the two parcels; it looks as though they are headed into the mainland of Madagascar within the next half hour if they can sustain swimming or if they have any injuries." Said one of the officers working on the computer data information obtained in live time.

"Perfect set the men up alongside the shoreline but not in full gear. We want to catch them by surprise. Make sure to give them the CPI monitors," Frank said over the intercom.

Within minutes the second batch of troops was deployed and on route to the location. Three suburban black unmarked vehicles drove in line to the area.

CHAPTER 31

Connemara got off the plane, her arm had its pulse from the pain. Nothing she could do now but hope that it would heal naturally since she didn't have the stone to reinforce healing quicker. The sun was hot, and it was a welcome change from the rain back home. She booked a vacation package at a reputable motel which supplied activities and excursions for the guests.

But Connemara was more interested in exploring the area. She had heard that some of her decedents originated here and Australia 100 years ago. In amongst the volcano veins hidden deep beneath the earth is when they discovered the earth's secret the Alexandrite stone.

She wanted to find someone who dealt with these stones and see if there was any way she could be set free from the family's heritage once and for all. "Hi, I am looking for something you have on the island where it's a native stone the Alexandrite? Would you be able to direct me to a jeweler or someone on the island that sells it?" Connemara's accent was pretty predominant and the local merchant rather than directing her felt a very strong connection and decided to inquire as to the motives behind the question.

The man she was talking to was Emerald; he still had not fully gotten back to his old self. He could tell by her eyes that something was familiar about the way her eyes twinkled. It reminded him of his daughters.

"Why, be such a young thing, want to know about such a stone? You can get it at any shop around town, why are you asking me?" Emerald coughed as he was eyeing her left arm which was bleeding through her freshly changed band-aids.

"Oh, well, I am studying it in school, and I am taken with them and wanted the best in the area so I figured instead of asking a tour guide I would ask you a local here. Right? You are a local this is your stand?"

Connemara looked at the goods he was selling and admired the lovely beadwork bracelets he had on display among other items, fresh fish, dyed fabrics, tees, and coconut cups. "I that be my stand and you are no ordinary gal are you though? My name is Emerald. I know who you are by your name and the twinkle in your eye if you catch my drift." He smiled big and looked around to see if anyone was within earshot looked back at her, he held out his hand to shake it.

"Jeez, was I that easy to spot?" she said looking flustered.

"No, but I am one of you so I can see your gem in your eyes although it isn't very bright, I am an old man I have seen a lot of things in my life, and you better believe it when I know something I gonna say it." They both laughed.

"Indeed, you did, so now I can be honest with you, I want to be free of this curse of managing my island. I want to live and travel and go where I want. I want to know if somehow, I can reverse it or get it out of me so I can be normal. I figured I would come to the source to get some answers."

"Well, ya come, to the right place this is where a few of them people started many years ago, but it doesn't just end here though. There is no way to undo the gifts you have been given my dear. Why is your arm bleeding? You can't heal it yourself? Here let me see and I can help you." He reached over and tried to touch her arm.

She retracted, "I removed it so I cannot. I just want it to be gone."

He started coughing again and spit blood, "I don't know what's gotten into your young people these days, but you are so selfish you making everybody else sick, and you don't even realize what you doing."

Behind him, a man with a gun and cameo approached them and demanded they stick their hands in the air. A government officer was called to deploy from the energy surges in the area from the scientific headquarters in Jamaica. They got the call and at once deployed the men to seize them. Now both of them were in handcuffs and Emerald shook his head at her and said nothing.

CHAPTER 32

Ruby and Diamond were at the shore. Legs shaking, not wanting to go on anymore they dragged themselves and lay face down in the sand trying to catch their breath and get the strength to get up and move. The officers were behind one of the residential homes along the beach and spying on them with guns pointed at each of their heads. The laser accuracy could have easily killed them.

"On my word when I tell you I want an attack on all fronts, no letting them escape but back into the sea copy?" said the leading officer on the call.

"Copy," the others said.

Ruby rolled on her back looked up into the grey sky and coughed some water out of her lungs, "Diamond what are we going to do now? The government is after us. They know about us. How did this happen? Our lives as we know it are over."

Diamond spoke softly, "I always knew this day would come but when it would happen however I did not. In Australia, there is a place for us to be safe. It is where we migrated from. Jamaica is another place we can go which is where it had started too originally. We have to make it known that our kind is in danger somehow. I can read your thoughts, but I don't think we can warn everyone that way it would take too much of our strength to do it."

"GO GO GO!" The officers ran out from behind the bushes and ran towards Ruby and Diamond.

Ruby got up and with strength from out of nowhere went ahead to lunge after one of the officers. Punching him square in the jaw with her arms glowing red she knocked him out. Another from behind her grabbed her making her lose her balance and pinned her in the sand.

Her anger got the better of her as she began to glow her entire body for the first time and a great force pulled him off and sent him far out into the sea. She stood up once more and Diamond was being held down by two more officers.

One had his knee in the small part of her back and a gun pointed at her head.

Ruby became enraged, she held out her hand and the gun began to turn into dust. The men became afraid and backed away from Diamond. Diamond ran over to Ruby, "Ruby you need to calm down now you will overheat and hurt yourself. We are not meant to hurt people with it!"

But Ruby couldn't hear her, she was so angry she couldn't stop it. She put her other hand out and the man's eyes began to bulge out. She was causing him pain without touching his body. She was beginning to feel the true power of the gem's gifts but was not fully aware of how they were to be used.

"Stop Ruby!" Diamond screamed.

Ruby looked at the terror in her eyes and fought to stop herself from launching the rest of the men into the sea. Diamond looked over by the dock and saw two Yamaha watercrafts tied up.

"Come on, we need to get out of here," Diamond grabbed her sister's hand and went to them. Ruby went on and both fired them up. They revved the engines and took off going 80 kilometers an hour. Within seconds they were past where they swam from.

The machines were agile and very keen on the throttle. The waves of the sea were no match for the powerful machines that cut through like a knife. The waterspout and sound of them gave them away however and could be seen far off into the distance. Luckily, it was late in the evening and soon it would be dark.

Ruby slowed down and waved to Diamond to come closer. "What are we going to do now we can't stay on the water forever?"

"I know, if only we knew someone here who could help us get out of here. "Diamond was looking distraught. Ruby thought about it and remembered Charlie. "I know someone who can help us, but we need to get to a phone. Let's ride further down the shoreline and see if we can get to one somehow."

CHAPTER 33

Sue managed to sell all of her produce and was pleased to see an old friend. Jade was the same age as her hitting the wise years of eighty and still fit and full of life as she ever was. They grew up in the same village and managed to keep in touch after all these years.

Sue confided in her and asked if any strange things were happening within her family. They were both from a long line of original Jewel people and they had the same powers. Jade looked at her with a lifted eyebrow.

"Oh, well that is why I've come. We have to leave this place, my dear friend, something has happened. We have been discovered by the government. It will only be a matter of time before they capture us. It is because they know not of our powers and what we are, so they are frightened of it and want to seek it out."

"I felt something was off, and after Li passed away I knew the world was falling apart. I am not myself still and don't know what is happening to me I felt better this morning but am still not myself."

Sue rubbed her arm to comfort herself as he spoke. "I know I am not the same either."

They walked in silence as they noticed some flashing lights ahead of them. They looked at each other and decided that going through the valley just below the field of flowers would be best to avoid any attention.

They started heading towards the field when shouts could be heard off in the distance.

"They are here already by a dear friend," Jade spoke as her arms and feet began to glow.

"I am too old to run Jade I will stay but you can go faster than me I will distract them," Sue said as she stopped in her tracks.

"I will not leave you." And with that, she enveloped Sue with a soft green glow and they both vanished from where they were standing.

CHAPTER 34

Charlie answered the phone, "Hi beautiful I am so glad you called I was just thinking about you."

"Hi, that is so sweet of you. I am in a bit of a jam. My sister and I need a ride to the airport we are going to go on a little vacation together so I was wondering if it wasn't too much trouble if you could pick us up."

Charlie smiled, "Of course! I'm just finishing up with work I will come get you. But I thought you were already on vacation. Any way I will be there in an hour."

Ruby didn't answer him and gave him the location before hanging up. "Okay, we are all set Diamond. We just need to get to the airport and hopefully, we are not being flagged right now otherwise we won't be going anywhere. But we have to try and how else will we get there."

Diamond knew another way but figured that what she needed of Ruby would take a long time to perfect, and they didn't have time for that.

"There is another way, but since you have just come into your power, we won't be able to do it."

"What do you mean?" Ruby looked confused.

"I mean we can go from place to place without having to worry about physical modes of transportation. However, I have never been able to do it. But it is possible as it is one of our traits." Diamond said looking seriously at her.

"Oh wow, that is amazing." Ruby was surprised at just how much she never knew about this gift she'd been given.

"Yeah, well for now we need to figure out how to stay hidden. Come with me I saw an old shed a few houses back that we can hide in while we wait for the guy you called to come to get us." Diamond turned to go in the direction of it as Ruby followed looking back every so often to make sure they were not being followed.

CHAPTER 35

Frank looked at the screen and saw the light of the coastline still. "How did they manage to escape? We need them obtained now! Before they figure out just how powerful they are."

"Yes sir, but sir the one that glowed and hurt my men already you mean they could potentially do more damage than that?" Officer John, who managed to come back from the scene, was visibly shaken but didn't let his emotions get in the way of his job.

"Yes, from what I am seeing the energy they are producing is equivalent to powering that of a large city like New York possibly or Los Angelo's even more than that. They don't know what they have because she could have easily killed you without much thought."

Frank rubbed his chin which had fresh stubble. He hadn't shaved in the last 24 hrs., and he hadn't slept.

"Well, then I will get more men and set up a sting with a sniper if needed to take them out if necessary." John went and got the list of men for Frank to approve.

"We cannot and I must emphasize this fact, we cannot have them killed. We want to study them and use the power they have to our benefit so that would have to be the result if they are out of control."

Frank started to sweat at the thought of having to tell the president why an asset for a global energy source was killed. The thought of it sent his stomach in turmoil.

"Sir, we have calls coming in from all over the globe, in Jamaica, they managed to capture two of them. But in China, some just seemed to drop off the face of the earth. We can't seem to find where they are at this point the energy reading has simply vanished."

One of the officers, immersed in answering calls and rapidly jotting down messages, reacted swiftly as news spread to the critical areas highlighted by the loudest energy readings on the map.

"Dispatch the details regarding the two individu-
als who were apprehended. I want them secured
and promptly transferred to our secure facility. A
conventional jail setting won't suffice," Frank
commanded with unwavering authority.

John promptly made the necessary phone
calls, ensuring that the full might of the elite mil-
itary personnel would be mobilized and on-site
within the hour.

CHAPTER 36

Emerald sat in the jail and looked at Connemara who was frightened and sitting in the next cell. He walked over to her as she sat gently sobbing.

"Here now, I will get us out of this mess. I was just trying to get my strength back since I've been not well lately. Here." His hands lit up and he melted the bars between them.

Connemara looked at him with surprise and ran and hugged him. "I'm sorry."

"Alright, we haven't got time now for you crying. You still got time to make up for things so let me get us outta here and we will fix this mess."

Emerald went ahead to glow his entire body; with one quick arm movement he blew out the back of the jail cell wall. It exploded and fragments of rock flew in all directions hitting the parked cop cars in the parking lot which started their alarms going off. Dust and debris made it hard to see as Emerald and Connemara disappeared from the area. It was as if they vanished out of existence.

Emerald sat on his couch exhausted as his kids ran around the living room. Connemara was sitting in the chair next to him and smiled as the children laughed, played, and tried to get her to play hide and look for.

She admired their innocence and wished to go back to a simpler time when she had no worries in the world. Now, she realized she made a mistake coming here and putting these little ones in danger and Emerald's whole family and life would never be the same.

Neither would hers.

Seconds later barrage of bullets whizzed through Emerald's house and within seconds everyone was dead. The entire family was included in the death count. The news kept it hidden and reported instead that there were a home invasion and innocent bystanders including a tourist passing by the area who must have seen the robbers died as well and was found outside the victim's home. Not the first time the government bought the media off to keep them quiet.

CHAPTER 37

Ruby watched as the trees, in the distance, moved. She couldn't be sure if it was the wind or more government men. She kept alert and repeatedly looked at the time on her now cracked and condensation filled watch.

Surprisingly, it still worked.

"Diamond we have about five minutes before Charlie will be here, we better get moving to the main road otherwise we will miss him." Ruby looked at her sister who was nursing her arm which was remarkably more inflamed now than when she first showed her.

Frank was on the phone with the new group dispatched to the scene. "Listen I don't want any more deaths; I want them alive do you hear me? We just lost two in Jamaica we cannot afford to lose any more. Understood?"

"Yes sir." John was in the vehicle waiting to catch them if they evaded the rest of his men. It was dark now and no one was out, which was good. He did not want to oversee any civilian casualties with his watch.

Ruby and Diamond appeared from the shed; Ruby's eyes glowed as she scanned the dark alley on the right of them.

"All clear if we go now but there seems to be moving just down to the left of that red Honda civic parked in that driveway from what I can tell."

The house attached had a side door light on and it was just enough to see the color of the car. No other streetlights were on because of the storm it had knocked out a large area and most homes were without power.

The silence fell unpleasantly, weighty; almost tangible.

Diamond looked at her sister and grabbed her arm before venturing further.

"When the time comes, it may be necessary to act with malice but only if necessary. If it gets to that point, I will not stop you this time. I feel like we are now at war, and something is not right within me. I can feel our energies are depleting. People are dying so we must preserve what little we have left. "

Ruby understood she felt it too, a weakness growing within her. Within seconds of being out in the open, the officers were on top of them. The attack was swift as lightning; Diamonds aching shoulder hampered her movements.

She was unable to dodge the first officer who smashed her in the face with the butt of his gun. She fell like a stone and tumbled straight into the boots of another officer who expected her movements and kicked her hard in the stomach.

Ruby was busy trying to prevent the officer's fist from connecting to her cheek; he was too slow and managed to lose his balance as she rammed him into the side of his head with her fist. Looking back, she saw Diamond on the ground and officers hovering over her.

Within seconds Ruby was on the men surrounding her, she grappled with the men her entire body glowed red. She threw them as if they weighed nothing just far enough to lift Diamond off the ground. Ruby held on to her sister and closed her eyes as the men pointed the gun at them.

Shots fired as they dispersed leaving a cloud of red and dispersed behind them as Ruby used everything she had to get her sister out of there muttering the words 'lapillus populous' over and over. In the meantime, Charlie waited by the roadside where they were told to meet.

He didn't see them, so he got out of his vehicle to look at the sea while he waited for them. It was pitch dark and the half-moon high in the sky revealed figures on the beach. He watched in horror as he saw Ruby fight the officers and disappeared. He was in awestruck and frozen with amazement as he had never seen anything quite like it.

CHAPTER 38

Australia is the world's biggest producer opal and of diamonds who is also a major supplier of sapphire, ruby, emerald, garnet, topaz, and jade has also been mined in Australia. It is where everything started. It is where the Jewel people originated.

Opal was a lovely tall blonde-haired woman in her late forties. She worked for the government and did a lot of charity work. She was kind-hearted and a valuable asset to the business world in cutting fair deals and had a lot of influence on those within power.

As she drove home early from working all night on a deal to cut emissions and fossil fuels for the city of Canberra her eyes were heavy, and she had trouble staying awake. Picking up her fresh cup of coffee she sipped it and took her eyes off the road for a moment to enjoy the liquid energy she needed to get back.

A call came in on her phone; it was the president's confidant Dell.

"Hi there, yes, Dell, I did finish the proposal as asked. Oh, what? Okay, I will be right there."

She slammed on the brakes since no one else was around and did an illegal U-turn and headed back to the office just as the sun was rising. She put on her shades as it was coming into her window.

'It's always something,' she muttered to herself.

CHAPTER 39

Jade and Sue reappeared and fell to the ground, both wiped out from traveling the great distance to be here. It was hot and the sun was just starting to rise. They were off into a rocky part of the beach coves and there was little shade for them. Jade used a magical projection to see where they had to go.

Sue looked on with faint excitement as she remembered the ancient location of caves in her dreams. Gleaming sands and ripples made it feel like she had been here before. Jade's eyes sparkled in the sunlight as the view from the sun that was disconnecting from the sea appearing high into the sky was very majestic.

It had a pleasant romantic kind of feel to it, something she would have enjoyed to sit and watching. She didn't know when they would be able to see this view again with everything that was happening, so she remained silent for a few more seconds as Sue closed her eyes and tilted her head to the sun to soak it in.

"Sue we must go, it isn't safe here any-more." Jade had already accepted their fate as she got up dusted the beach sand off of her and helped her dear friend.

"I know, it was a good life we had, though I don't regret a thing. I only wish that Li could be here with me." Tears filled her eyes.

Jade never married so she did not know of the bond they shared but she knew she was in pain; she could feel it deep within her as all the Jewel people were connected in some way.

"Come, my sister, let us go into the cave and be rid of this mess." Jade held on to Sue and locked arms together as they trekked off in the direction of the mouth of the cave and disappeared into the shadows.

CHAPTER 40

Ruby and Diamond reappeared, and both lost their balance as they ended up in the middle of the main road. A car nearly swerved and hit them. Unable to move from exhaustion Ruby looked over at Diamond.

"Diamond, are you okay?" Ruby shook Diamond and found that she was unresponsive. She held her in her arms and lifted her to her chest. "Diamond? Diamond, please wake up!" Ruby was much louder now as pedestrians were starting to gather around them.

Ruby noticed her hands were wet and looked at them. She was covered in Diamond's blood. She screamed and moved her back onto the ground to try and find where it was coming from. She turned to her side and saw the blood from the back of her head had sustained a single bullet and had been bleeding down her back as they traveled.

Ruby didn't care who was around her she quickly tried to heal her. She put her hand on the wound and went ahead to glow from her arms to her toes. The crowds around her gasped and stood back as they watched her try to heal her sister.

It was too late.

By now Opal had gotten out of her car and ran over to them. "Dear God, what have I done? Did I hit her back there? I didn't feel anything. Please I must get you both to the hospital." Opal was beside herself as she looked at Ruby's glowing red body which didn't seem to scare her at all.

Ruby looked up to the heavens as if someone from above could help her and let out a scream of frustration and remorse. Hot fiery tears ran down her face. The skies turned black, and the wind picked up as fire pellets ran down from the heavens. Ruby was enraged by her selfishness, how could I let this happen she thought. Her sister was killed, and it was her fault.

Opal looked at Ruby and understood, she touched her arm gently and a pearl-like glow softly lit her hand as she helped her up. "We must go; I will help you carry her to my car. We cannot leave her here."

Ruby was in shock and didn't speak further. People in the crowd were taking pictures and scattered when the fire pellets started. They bounced easily off of the women as they carried Ruby's dead sister to the backseat of Opal's car.

CHAPTER 41

Charlie had been taken into custody when the men saw him standing there watching the events unfold. They extricated him for 24hrs, but he did not reveal that he knew the woman he just happened to be in the area and heard a noise while out for a stroll that evening and was completely innocent.

But the government had already traced his whereabouts and knew he was lying.

"So, you're telling me, the woman on the plane that you sat next to for over 5hrs and just happened to be at the same place that night was a coincidence?"

John was tired and had enough of this whole thing. He was not even sure he wanted to do this anymore. Those women looked terrified when he caught a glimpse of them just before they vanished.

"I AM TELLING YOU I DON'T KNOW WHO SHE WAS!" Charlie was getting frustrated and raised his voice to make it crystal clear. He needed answers himself, but he knew for certain that Ruby could not be evil or a monster like they made it out to be.

"Throw him into the cell. I need to get clearance from Frank before we can let him go." John spoke to the other officer who was in front of the door guarding the entrance to the interrogation room.

Frank was on the phone with the Chinese embassy, shit was hitting the fan. Major environmental events were taking place in China, and they just experienced a large tsunami, and it killed over a hundred thousand civilians.

There was a lot of shouting and okay's coming from the direction of Franks back as he had it faced toward his office which he could not get to in time for the incoming phone call. "Yes, I perfectly understand sir, but I am not aware of where the energies went after they reappeared in Australia. So, they must have died, or something cause otherwise, it would be impossible. They are nowhere sir; trust me we have looked. I am aware of their capabilities to travel undetected, but it's been too long now, and nothings showed up anywhere."

Frank slammed the cell on the table and leaned over on the desk.

"I think us chasing them is causing the global weather conditions lately. I can't put my finger on it but ever since we started chasing these things these people everything has been going haywire. Jamaica is having for the first time in a hundred years a volcanic eruption killing thousands of civilians now China..." his voice trailed off as he looked at the weather news taking place on the television monitor in Australia "Reporting Fire pellets from the sky and people were scattered about running for their lives in terror."

CHAPTER 42

Opal drove Ruby and Diamond to the hospital and stopped outside the entrance. She didn't shut the car off as she looked and decided what to do.

"We can't go in with her we will have to leave her here." Opal looked at Ruby as she spoke, who looked deflated and defeated and just wanted to cry.

"I am so sorry. I didn't even ask your name. My name is Opal. I Figured yours is Ruby from the look of things I saw out there in the middle of the road back there. That and I could see the jewels in your eyes. You are like me; I wasn't sure I would ever meet another of my kind. My parents told me there were others but..."

Ruby cut her off.

"This is all my fault you know. I didn't get my jewel when I was supposed to, and all of this is because of me. My sister is dead and I'm sure there are others by now; the government is chasing us to figure out who we are. And now everyone is in danger including you. I don't know how to fix this."

"Ah, I see. Well, there has to be a way to fix this. I know that because we have been around for centuries, and we will continue to be. We just have to convince them that we aren't evil we do well for the world and help protect it. Maybe if I spoke to someone, I work at the government office, and we can resolve this quite easily. People are always afraid of the unknown."

Opal started to drive away and left her sister to remain in the backseat.

Ruby looked off into the distance. "No, they want to study us and find out how to get our power. That is what they want. They don't care how because at the end of the day it's all about power and money."

"I can agree there are a lot of corrupt people in government, but I am not one of them. We should at least try, right? I can call from an encrypted phone, and they won't know our location and I will explain everything to them. They know me and trust me. This will all go away once I tell them." Opal was always very optimistic, and this was no time to change now.

Opal turned the corner and saw a police officer ahead of her. The light was red, and Opal gave space between her car and his. The officer looked into his rearview and looked down then looked again. Opal began to get nervous as the officer put on his lights and tried to get out of his car.

Without thinking about it she put her foot on the gas and floored it, went into oncoming traffic, and swerved nearly missing an old lady carrying some grocery bags. She sped the car and cornered the next street just barely kissing the curb. Ruby grabbed on to the handle above her and held on.

"Hang on," Opal called out as she weaved in and out between cars that were honking at her as she passed them and managed to go under an overpass that was still under construction as she screeched to a halt.

The workers were not working on it due to the weather.

"Well, this is going to prove a bit more difficult if they already are looking for us. I need to get to the office and get my phone to call the president's secretary." Opal was rummaging through her purse looking for something.

"They keep finding me no matter where I go it seems. It's like they have a tracker on me. I am sorry to get you involved. Do they know you are like me? I wonder." Ruby bit her bottom lip for the first time. She was concerned for another person besides herself and her family. She didn't want anyone else getting hurt. She had to do something to protect them.

CHAPTER 43

Charlie rubbed his wrists as they finally let him go. The handcuffs were too tight and felt like his circulation was being cut off. He was told to get on a plane and go back home at once. He realized that he was being followed once he left the building. But once he got on the plane, he didn't see anyone else who seemed suspicious and looked like a government agent.

He was glad they let him go but they kept his cell for evidence under suspension and told him not to return to Madagascar again. It would be on his official passport information should he feel brave and think he can in the future.

"Where are you, Ruby?" He said out loud to himself as he looked out the window of the plane taking off for California. The clouds had not returned to blue skies and the weather was unusual. It was colder than it should have been, and the wind had picked up.

The captain over the intercom said it was going to be a bumpy ride with a lot of turbulence as the weather was bad. Charlie didn't give it a second thought he hadn't slept yet and hoped to put this unpleasant experience behind him and get some desperately needed sleep.

Perhaps when he got back, he could look up Ruby's family's last name and see if any relatives lived near him that he would be able to find her. But for now, he settled in and asked for a blanket and pillow from the flight attendant.

Frank told John he could let Charlie go on the condition that he is followed. He wanted to know his every movement and hoped that he would lead them to Ruby since he knew Charlie was lying. It was too coincidental that they were in the same location that evening and if his hunch proved right this would all be over soon.

"John, put an agent on Charlie. He is to follow him wherever he goes. And, for god's sake don't lose him! He is our only chance to get those women. Who knows even lead us too more of them?" Frank was trying not to sound so desperate in his voice as he spoke, but time was running out and people in high places were wanting his head on a platter if they didn't get results soon.

Frank looked at the world map and saw the light had come up again in Australia. "What the hell!"

He looked over at the others who were watching the energies that were significantly less now.

"Why didn't anyone inform me that there was large energy now in Australia? I need to know these things as soon as it occurring people!" He slammed his fist on the table and picked up the phone.

"Get me the president's secretary of Australia now!"

CHAPTER 44

Ruby felt a lump in her back pocket as she remembered her journal was still with her. She took it out again and opened the last few pages.

September 10, 1976

All is well now that I have the jewel in my possession.

I remember a lot of things that I could not remember before. I know now of the locations of ancient places and the caves of many places where others have appeared from.

For it is known that we are not alone but we are connected as one unit, one entity, a joined collaboration of people who protect the earth from harm and keep the balance of nature and all of those around us.

And just as this information has come to me so it will for you. I fear that if this gets into the wrong hands there would be a global disaster so therefore, I will not write what I know but say this.

"Debemus praesidio alli" (we must protect others)

Ruby closed the book and her eyes as she tried to remember more about what could help her now. A flood of memories flashed as she saw people drinking the crushed rubies, diamonds, and other precious jewels.

She saw maps, various places, and her mother's face that smiled at her and told her that she had the power to fix it all, but she would need to believe it. Ruby opened her eyes and looked at Opal who managed to find candy at the bottom of her purse and was eating it, deep in thought also.

"I know where we need to drop Diamond off. I need you to take us there right now."

Opal smiled and said, "I know I just saw the image you saw. We are connected more than we know it seems."

CHAPTER 45

Charlie got back to his bachelor apartment late that night. The flight was awful he didn't sleep a wink and at times thought they would crash. He tossed and turned in his sleep as he kept having visions of Ruby in danger and felt the urge to help her but every time he went to she slipped through his fingers like sand. He sat up and looked at his clock. 1 am and he was now overtired.

He went to his computer and looked up Ruby's last name, Lapis.

"Huh, that's ironic," Charlie muttered out loud, Lapis, meant stone in Latin and her first name was also one.

Could just be a coincidence, he thought.

A few addresses came up; one was just 133 kilometers away. He grabbed some coffee and headed out, by the time he would get there it would be morning anyway and he couldn't sleep until he knew more anyway.

The sun was supposed to be coming up, but it was grey here too which was odd for sunny California. He parked outside the house and waited for a decent time to go knocking on this person's door. He listened to the weather, and it was reporting a severe thunderstorm in effect for today.

The time on his car clock said 8:30 am which was still early he thought until he saw an older gentleman take his dog out for a morning pee. He got out of the car and approached him.

"Hi, excuse me. Sorry for bothering you so early in the morning but I was wondering if you happened to know a Ruby Lapis? I know you don't know me, and it is strange of me to visit this early but if you don't mind can I speak to you inside? I would rather not talk about it out in the open."

"That sounds very cryptic my dear man, but I haven't seen or heard from her in a while, and I am growing increasingly worried so I will humor you and it looks as though you could use some coffee and breakfast."

Ruby's father said as he held the door open for him to go inside. Gizmo ran in ahead of them both and wagged his tail as Charlie jumped up and sat next to him on the couch.

"Thank you, I appreciate it, I met your daughter on a plane to Madagascar last week and we hit it off. She is an amazing woman. I got very fond of her quite quickly. Our encounter however brief was startled by something I saw a few days later. I know it is going to sound crazy, but I need you to hear me out."

Charlie's palms were getting sweaty, and Gizmo decided now was the perfect time to jump on his lap and lick his face.

"Oh, I have heard of some strange things in my day, continue." Ruby's dad was making fried egg sandwiches and a pot of freshly brewed coffee.

Outside, the agent pulled up behind Charlie's car. He called into frank to tell him the information before inquiring if he should wait until he left to ask questions about why he was there at all.

"That is the father of the person we are looking for, lay low and wait to see what he does afterward. Don't do anything now because we haven't found her yet. We want any information, and the father would be the one to know anything."

Frank hung up. The agent drove off to the end of the street turned the car around and shut it off. After they ate and Charlie finished telling Ruby's father about what had happened, they sat in silence.

Ruby's dad got up and paced, "Well she is definitely in danger and her sister too. I knew something was wrong I just couldn't put my finger on it. I have no way of contacting her either. I've tried several times on her cellphone, but I figured that being in that part of the world in the jungle she would be hard to reach, anyway."

Charlie felt like he was avoiding something. "How can you explain what I saw, I mean she disappeared out of nowhere. And, those men, they were trying to hurt her, but she was so strong... I've never seen anything like it."

"I have, my wife was just like Ruby is now. Strong, fearless. Listen I don't know exactly what you thought you saw but I can tell you this. We need to find her before those men do. I doubt however she is still in Madagascar either. She will reach out I'm sure to both of us once she is somewhere safe. In the meantime, get some rest."

Gizmo sighed and put his head on Charlie's lap and automatically he rubbed the dog's head. He looked at his collar and saw a blue gem around his neck. "What a beautiful and unusual collar you have."

"It was my late wife's... Anyway, I have some things I need to do today so I think it's time we parted ways."

And, with that Ruby's dad opened the front door and escorted Charlie out.

CHAPTER 46

Frank was sweating in his office; the temperature had gone up and even the air conditioner was working hard to keep the place from roasting. It was a whopping 120 Fahrenheit the hottest on record to date. He loosened his tie and put on his fan on his desk. The local news was having a field day as there was plenty of news to go around.

Sudden forest fires were popping up all over the city as firefighters scrambled to put them out. The air was thick with humidity and smoke making it impossible to stay outside for very long. There was an increasingly alarming rate of continual warnings about venturing outside for any length of time on the television and cellphones kept going off to remind people of the dangers with government localized texting.

"John, do we any updates on the Australian government updating them on the present situation? I would like to have eyes and ears over there, but we need probable cause, and it would help matters if we could get some of that video footage from the residents of anything unusual."

"Yes, sir I just spoke to the agent that we have on Charlie. He just spoke to her father. I am requesting permission to interrogate the father on a home lockdown. The agent is prepared and has checked on him all day. He is alone with one small dog. No one other than Charlie has come to visit him."

John cleared his throat. It was sore from the smoke inhalation when he drove in this morning. The air was coming in despite his windows staying closed and air conditioning on full blast.

"We don't have any authority to be doing anything just yet. I need the go-ahead from the chief of the defense force to have free reign. They are not convinced that these women are of any threat to the country, so they have not approved it."

"What would you like me to tell him?" John held the phone away from his ear.

"Tell him if he gets caught, he no longer works for us." Frank walked back into his office and shut the door.

CHAPTER 47

Ruby carried Diamond easily. Her frail life-less body of the woman whom she grew up with was no more. Tears streamed down her face as they walked from the parking lot of the beach to the rocky shores. Opal remained silent they both knew where to go. They had clear visions of it, and this was the only proper burial for her.

Ruby looked back to make sure they were not being followed. It was late in the evening, and they had been driving for most of the day and somehow managed to avoid any more officers on the road. They came to a built-up cavernous area just off the main beach and turned into the sunset and walked into the shallow waters.

Rock formations from small to large scat-tered the area and one very large one which looked to be sparkling amongst the rest was tall and elegant. They headed around it and were hid-den now from the beach and the only ones who could have seen them would have been boaters, but no one was out in this heat.

Ruby went in ahead of Opal and found the dark entrance that was unnoticeable to humans because their eyes were not meant to see it. Only those who had the jewels powers could. They disappeared to the naked eye into the rock and vanished.

They walked down deep into the underground caverns; they were underneath the sea now and the smell of the sea air was as fresh and clean as it meant to, and it came from within. Far away from outside, safe from the natural disasters from the government and from people they would be safe here.

Ruby carried her sister for more than 100 miles before a light in the distance could be seen. As they walked in silence the light became blinding to them. They continued and stepped through to the red-hot pool that set the tone in the middle of the entrance. The lava dripped like a waterfall and gently arrived at the pool keeping it replenished.

They were home.

There were more of those ancient symbols on the walls as they decorated the area; the gems were laid on the walls of all kinds, Diamonds,

Emeralds Ruby's, and Safire's which glittered and danced as they reflected the lava's light. Everything they needed was also there for them, food, beds, and freshwater.

It looked as though someone was there recently. Opal put her finger to her lips as she looked at Ruby and went off deeper still into the cavern which was hollowed out many years ago. Ruby gently put Diamond on one of the beds and sat down at the end of the bed. She covered her face and began to cry. Opal returned with Jade to her surprise she jumped back and was startled. She was lost in her grief and didn't hear them approach.

"I am sorry, I startled you, my child. I see you must be in a lot of pain. I too am in pain. My beloved friend has passed shortly after we got here. My condolences to you for your loss."

Jade spoke softly to her. Ruby wiped her eyes.

"Thank you, we must bury her here. I don't want anyone digging her up to do experiments on her. That is why we have come."

"My child we will make a beautiful place-
ment for her next to my Sue. Come I will show
you. We have much to discuss."

Jade took her hand and lead her to the
graves while she spoke to her in her native
tongue.

CHAPTER 48

Onyx, a young man in his early twenties, embarked on a journey to Brazil to obtain his stone as a rite of passage upon reaching his twentieth birthday. Possessing a striking appearance, he had a head of black hair that complemented his darker skin tone, displaying a lovely olive complexion. Standing at an impressive six feet tall, Onyx often found himself towering over others, prompting him to adopt a slight slouch to appear less intimidating.

Despite his imposing stature, Onyx's disposition resembled that of a large teddy bear. Known for his kind-hearted nature, he didn't harbor a mean bone in his body. However, his physique spoke volumes about his commitment to fitness, as his well-defined muscles attested to a dedication to self-care. Working at a construction site, Onyx reveled in the satisfaction of building things with his own hands, a passion that resonated with his demeanor.

Lately, things didn't feel quite right, and he felt like the world was coming to an end. When watching the news every evening after work while he ate a large meal, he noticed the escalation of environmental disasters.

Last Friday, there was a black sedan parked across the street from his custom-built house he himself built with his own two hands. He looked out the window and noticed it was parked there again and a man was inside. He glanced at the time, deciding to confront the man. He went out the back way and went behind the bushes so he could catch whoever was off guard. He was at the back of the sedan and overheard the man on the phone.

"Nothing unusual here. I will wait until dark. I am aware of the consequences sir. Yes, sir ten four."

The agent was looking at his half-eaten bagel contemplating if he was going to toss it out the window or finish it. Onyx crept up alongside the vehicle and just like the character in pop goes the weasel, he popped his head in front of the side window, startling the driver.

"Hi there. I noticed you have been parked in front of my house for the last week and I'm wondering what you are doing, just out of curios-ity?"

The man slammed open the car door which knocked Onyx to the ground and before he could get up the car sped away. Onyx stood up and brushed himself off as the car screeched around the corner.

Charlie, a neighbor, came outside to see what the commotion was about.

"Hey man, what happened?" Charlie trying to be hip said to the young man brushing off his shorts.

"Oh hey, some guy has been parking outside across my house for the last week, I asked what he was doing here, and then he pushed his car door open and drove away. What a weirdo."

Charlie got nervous. "Oh, right yeah, that's strange."

Onyx gave him a puzzled look. "You, okay? It's dark out but looked like you just went all pale, man. Do you know that guy or something? Are you in some kind of trouble?"

"Um... me? NOOOO no, ahem," clearing his throat. "I am fine really. I should get back in-side. Well, it was nice talking to you... I didn't catch your name dude."

Onyx chuckled, "I didn't give out my name but since it appears we are neighbors, I'm Onyx."

"Huh, what an unusual name that is. I have been meeting a lot of people with Jewels for names lately." Charlie slipped it out and regretted saying it as soon as it did.

Onyx looked at him with puzzled brows. "Okay then, well it was nice meeting you?"

"Sorry, it's Charlie."

"Okay, Charlie was super nice meeting you. I'm going to go have my dinner now. Peace." Onyx gave him the peace sign with his fingers shook his head and laughed while he walked back into his house.

"Yeah... you too!" Charlie waved but he wasn't looking.

CHAPTER 49

Ruby's father Brad was getting more and more concerned for his daughters. The pet dog Gizmo who didn't seem interested in the one-sided conversation he was having with him gently started to snore.

"Well thanks very much for your help Gizmo; I was trying to talk to you, you old mutt." He chuckled to himself.

He looked at the collar and rubbed it and thought about the girls when they were young and all the dreams, he had for them. He knew one day they would become very important but at what cost? He put on the outside light and wandered off to the bedroom. His window was still open a little and he could smell the smoke that had drifted from the valley was still very strong. He decided to close it all the way.

The agent was behind the bed lying flat on the floor. He had a tranquilizer needle filled with a clear liquid that would put the man out for an hour while he set up the house, input the government bug system to the phones and tie him up to the chair and ask him a series of questions.

He was on his own now, no help from Frank or John. But he wanted a name for himself, and this was the only way to get some recognition before he retired for good. He was a retired cop who got his badge of honor for saving his fellow partner's life and was asked to the secret service shortly after.

His name was old school Walter after his late uncle on his father's side. He waited for the man to turn the corner and grabbed his leg throwing him to the ground. He took out the needle and jabbed it into his calf as he tried to scramble to get up. Within a second's movement stopped but Gizmo was barking and growling at Walter now and seemed to be foaming at the mouth.

"Easy their fella, I'm not gonna hurt you. Shhh."

Gizmo was small and old but something the man didn't know was that he was wearing the Jewel collar that gave him strength and healed him from his arthritis. The dog lunged onto the bed and turned to face him. Mouth foaming, teeth barred he went after the man's jugular and bit into his flesh knocking the man down and tripping over Ruby's father who was still knocked out.

He ripped it into the man's throat and punctured the artery. The man gasped, gagged, and tried to stop the bleeding at his throat. The dog bit him repeatedly in the face and didn't stop until the man fell silent. The dog then went over to Brad, lay beside him, and wept for him to wake.

CHAPTER 50

The Onyx is a traditional black gemstone. The black onyx stone is believed to absorb and transform negative energy and it also prevents the personal drain of one's own energy.

The black Onyx also aids in the development of emotional and physical strength especially in times of dire need. Because of these healing properties and their incredible power, it faired even more when paired with other precious stones.

Onyx was unaffected by the draining of energies around him from the other, Lapis people. He was a separated entity and one of the newest in the tribes of ancient lapillus populus generations. His generation of family members thrived for many centuries as one to be sought out in times of dire need.

The others when the tragedies of life happened used them as doctors to aid in healing but not as the cure but as a force of healing to help others. Charlie got up early and looked out his window. He saw Onyx getting into his Dodge extended cab dual rear tire cherry red truck and got back out again. Charlie got dressed quickly and ran out the door.

He decided on a wild idea to follow him. It was too weird his name was a jewel too and he couldn't help but think that there could be some connection with all this. Onyx waved at Charlie as he opened his front door. Onyx didn't stop for pleasantries, however. Got into his truck and drove off. Charlie went to the end of his driveway to see which way he was turning.

Once he saw him ran to his car and peeled out of the driveway nearly hitting Onyx's mailbox before throwing it into drive and leaving tire tracks in front of the house. Charlie looked in his rearview mirror and saw the same black sedan from the night before two cars behind him.

"Shit," Charlie muttered.

Onyx's truck stood out like a sore thumb, and it was easy to see him up ahead. There were three cars in between him and the truck. It was about a twenty-minute ride until he realized he had followed him to work.

Charlie pulled over and waited for Onyx to park his truck. The black sedan parked at the end of the street. Charlie decided that this was becoming an increasingly stupid idea and his rumbling tummy seemed to agree with him.

It was so loud it was distracting, so distracting he started to rummage in his glove compartment hoping there was a granola bar or gum or something that could tie him over until he decided to figure out what his next move was.

His cellphone rang from an unknown caller. *My boss,* he thought.

He hadn't gone back to the office since he came back into town and imagined they wanted an update on the real estate properties.

He looked at his phone contemplating answering it when he heard a gentle tapping on his window of the driver's side door. He looked up and Onyx was looking at him, not in a friendly way either. Charlie smiled at him and unrolled his window.

"Eh... how's it going?" Charlie's voice was shaken but trying to sound casual.

"I don't know, why don't you tell me? You followed me to work this morning and I'm not sure why so maybe you can explain that to me and the sedan at the end of the street. I am guessing he's for you?"

Onyx was angry and not hiding it.

"Um well I can explain but it would sound completely nuts."

Charlie didn't know how to explain it to himself let alone anyone else.

"Try me." Onyx was not leaving until he figured out why his neighbor was following him.

Charlie sighed, looked back at the sedan, and decided to come clean.

"I will but you have to come for a drive with me I can't explain it otherwise. Besides, we have company, and I am assuming that they would not want me talking to anyone about it so this is the only choice I can give you."

"Alright give me a few minutes I am going to tell my boss I will need to take a few hours off." Onyx walked away disappeared around the corner and came back with two steaming hot coffees from the trailer he emerged from.

"I know it's hot as sin out, but I figured with that morning breath you are sporting you didn't have time to eat or have coffee." Onyx laughed as he slid not too easily into the front seat of his car handing him the other coffee.

"Thanks." Charlie appreciated it and turned red from embarrassment.

CHAPTER 51

The three women filled each other in on what had taken place over the last few days and sat in silence as they drank some of Jade's Chia tea she made.

"You know I can't stay here." Opal finally broke the silence. Ruby looked at Jade and then Opal.

"Why not? There is nothing out there for is anymore." Jade piped up.

Ruby thought about all that had happened and the deaths of hundreds of people, now possible in the thousands with the natural disasters taking place.

"We have to go back and help those people. It is our duty and our birthright. We have to protect our areas, but I cannot think of a way to stop the government from trying to hunt us down like animals. And now that they have the technology to find us we cannot escape once we are back in the open. I am open to suggestions if anyone can think of something."

Opal looked at her watch. Time seemed to have slowed down since they entered the cavern because she could have sworn, they were there for hours.

"I work for the government as I said before and I talk with the president's confidant all the time. We have a good relationship. I think the best way to get them to back off is if we can show them that our presence is vital to save the planet from self-destruction. It is worth a shot at least but I will need time and a distraction."

Ruby thought about it.

"A distraction? Hmm well, I can make my-self known and get them to come to me while you go and get a hold of whomever you need to speak to. But if they catch me and nothing is done beforehand, I will be dead."

Jade started to speak. "It is very noble to put your life in jeopardy Ruby but if they kill any more of us there won't be enough of us to be able to continue to protect the earth. You must under-stand that they have brought this on themselves, and my dear friend is gone. I never bore children so I will not pass on the responsibility to another.

"I don't know how many are left of us if I am honest, I fear that the numbers are dropping as my strength is now weak even now as I sit in this place my jewel flickers as if it is about to go out. And I am okay with that, I have lived a long life, and I am content to go in peace."

Ruby checked her stone on her arm as she lifted her sleeve to see as Opal did. Both were bright and filled the cave with their stones light.

"I believe we can do this and there is so much more of us than you think Jade. But I don't want you to leave this place just yet. I want you to stay here and see if you can find more of us by using your abilities to see into others as you did with me. I felt you probing my mind a long time ago. I know it is you because as soon as you spoke, I recognized your voice. You have a gift of true sight – a third eye if you want to see into the window of others. Am I wrong?" Ruby looked her dead in the eyes.

"I haven't done that in years, so many years. When I was a much younger woman, I had those abilities. I feel like it was a violation to pry into one's mind, so I stopped. That and it drains my energy." Jade looked down at her wrinkled aged hands and rubbed them as if they were in pain.

Opal spoke now. "Listen she may not need to, if I can convince them then we will be able to use that information to find others. If I can make them understand then..." Her voice trailed off thinking of how she would explain she was also one of them.

Ruby was deep in thought. "I have an idea."

CHAPTER 52

Brad woke up with a wicked headache. His vision was a little blurred as he tried to get up. Gizmo was on his chest kissing him all over.

"Okay boy, calm down I'm alright."

He patted him on the head and noticed his hands were sticky. He looked at his hands as he wiped them on his pants and saw the dark liquid on them.

"What the hell?" He looked over at the man who put the needle in his leg lying there with his face half chewed off and his neck full of puncture holes.

"Oh my god!" He felt a hot flash come over him and he vomited on the man as he gripped the side of the bed for balance.

The dog jumped on the bed and tried to lick him again. "No Gizmo let's get you cleaned up first."

The phone rang while he was bathing Gizmo. Still not sure of what he would do about the man in his bedroom who died from his daughter's old Pug dog. In which he thought was an assassin of sorts and a slight hero since he did protect him.

It was 11 am when he looked at the time. He must have been out for a long time he thought as he absent-mindedly picked up the phone.

"Hi there, it's Charlie. We met the other day. I was wondering if you heard anything from Ruby."

Brad remembered, "Yes, I remember you. I have something here that may belong to you. I think you should come and grab it before I call the police and have you arrested young man!"

"What? I am sorry I don't follow what you're saying. I have someone with me, so I am not sure if it's okay if I bring him along. I need to verify something for him if that's okay."

Charlie's head hurt from having to spend the morning explaining himself to Onyx and now Brad was acting strange.

"At this point, I will not be here within the next couple of hours. There has been a change of plan and I have decided to go away to my cabin near the lake and check to see if it's still standing. SO, I won't be home but I will leave the door open for you so you can take this out of here and clean up."

Brad was mad and didn't want any part of this man's troubles. There was no way his daughter was going to be involved with that man as far as he was concerned.

"Umm, okay? Well, if I can get there soon then I will stop in." Charlie was even confused.

Onyx was in the passenger seat still and refused to leave until he had answers and proof that Charlie wasn't some mental case, and that the government was following him.

"You seem a little off from that phone call. Is everything alright?"

"Yeah, we just have to hurry because he's leaving for some reason now, so we have to catch him before he goes out of town." Charlie put his foot on the gas and sped up. Charlie's cell went off. It was an unknown number. He hesitated to pick it up. "Hello?"

"Hi there, it's me." The voice said in a soft tone.

Charlie slammed on the brakes and pulled over. Onyx grabbed onto the dashboard. "Whoa, man!"

"Where are you? I need to see you. No. I will as soon as I am done, I will come to you. When? Okay. Listen, please be safe." Charlie hung up.

"That was cryptic, who was that?" Onyx was curious.

"It's her."

CHAPTER 53

Andry was deep in the Jamaican jungle when he found what he was looking for. Embedded in the side of the rock exactly where Safire said it would be. He never thought he would be here, and it would come to this. But he never forgot what she said about the Alexandrite stone. He chipped off a large chunk and put it into his backpack and returned to the hotel.

He made the last flight before the warnings hit and now, he was desperate to get off the island. The volcano was smoking and made the surrounding skies black. It rained ashes and was dangerous to be there. He kept checking with the hotel clerk if any word on planes leaving for California was available but nothing so far.

He went to his room and removed the stone from his bag. He flipped it in his hands as it sparkled in the lamplight. "So much trouble this world. I hope this helps Safire." He said out loud and flipped on the news.

The volcano had erupted, and the other side of the island was now engulfed in lava and hundreds of thousands of homes were now charred and burned to a crisp. It was only a matter of time before the rest of the island would become uninhabited. People were leaving by boat and making shifting rafts in desperation to escape the island.

The phone in his room rang and he leaped for it. "Yes?" Oh, thank god. Yes, I am ready. I will be down in five minutes."

They were evacuating the island and help was on the way. Other countries were lending planes and cruise ships to gather the residents and whoever was left. The sky was even darker now and ashes were falling heavier. It was hard to see. The bus driver had to put his wipers on fast to keep up with it. People were terrified, crying, and children were screaming.

Andry sat on the back of the bus; it was going to transfer them to a cruise ship in the area that was coming to port. The roads were unkempt, and it was a very bumpy ride. Women were holding rosaries and had bibles in their hands. The bus swerved suddenly and went off of the road.

"Hold on Everyone!" The driver said as they crashed into small bushes and trees nearly avoiding a head-on collision with a large coconut tree.

"The lava has reached this road I'm gonna have to find another way there!" he yelled and tried to talk over the top of the crying women and children.

The ashes turned into hot lava raindrops as it burned on the top of the roof of the bus and was making visible indents on the inside of the bus. Trees were starting to go on fire and smoke was unbearable. "Roll up the windows! We must keep the smoke out! The men who were on the bus got up and started to close the windows as the women tried to calm the children.

The coughing and choking on the smoke that made it in the bus made Andry's eyes water. He was starting to wonder if they would make it to the ship. All of a sudden, the bus tipped on its side and threw the passengers and Andry to the other side of the bus.

Screaming and smashing into each other caused a lot of injuries. Smoke started to fill the inside of the bus. The driver was unconscious. Andry searched for his bag and threw it on his back. He had to push his way over people to get to the front of the bus. He shook the driver, but he was lifeless.

"Everyone we need to get out of here and stay under the trees!" Andry's voice boomed.

Not everyone listened but he didn't have time to waste.

"IF you stay here you will die! You must come now. If one of the fires catches the fuel it will blow you all to pieces! Please hurry and get off the bus."

Andry pushed the lever on the front door of the bus, and it opened. He climbed out and started to help the other passengers one by one. Children were passed to him first, women and then the men. As soon as the remaining men started to climb out the bus started to become inflamed.

"Hurry! Faster we must go now!" Andry was exhausted but he pushed on. The hot ashes burned through his clothing and hit his face and head. It happened. The bus exploded which threw him 10 feet in the air. Those passengers tried to get out were instantly killed.

Andry didn't hear anything but a loud ringing noise as he hit the ground with a thud. His Backpack was still on his back as it helped to break his fall, but it knocked the wind out of him. Some people ran over to him to check on him. He couldn't get up. They lifted him and with one person on either side holding him up by the shoulder. They quickly went back into the covering of the trees and pushed on to hopefully make it in time to meet with the ship.

The passengers had scrapes and burns but made it to the shore. They dropped Andry into the tree to rest as they waved for the ship! Smaller dingy boats appeared and came to shore and gathered them in sets of three full boats at a time. Andry was the last to be picked up. He had to be carried. He sustained many third-degree burns, and his arms and hands were raw with cuts and bruises.

Finally, off of the island, safe for now as the passengers watched their beloved home engulfed in flames and the red glow off in the distance as the island was taken over by hot molten rock.

CHAPTER 54

Frank watched the YouTube video that had mysteriously surfaced showing Ruby and Diamond on the shore fighting the men.

"God damn it! Find the source of this video and put a stop to it now!"

He walked into his office and slammed the door. The last thing he needed was the media having a field day with this. The phone rang and Dell was on the phone.

"I hear you have reason to believe there are quote UN quote beings or energies in our country and are considered dangerous? Rest assured we will be taking over that as you have no reason to be here or any of your men. And, let me forewarn you, Frank that the president is not pleased knowing there are agents here already which he did not clear with the secret service."

"It was a misunderstanding sir we simply wanted to ensure that the person in question was not going to blow up the president's home or something." Frank undid the top button on his shirt as he nervously spoke.

"Bullshit Frank! You get whoever you got in our country out of here until further notice. We will manage it. I would however love to see the tech you have for how you are tracking this so-called source. Since you seemed to have given it to other scientific environmental facilities except for Australia! You are creating a powerful enemy by doing business this way." Dell was furious as he spoke.

"Dell, you misunderstood, we have every intention of giving you the tech we ran into a bit of a problem, and it was delayed. That's all. So, we will send that information and equipment as soon as possible. Please forgive America for our error." Frank knew he was lying through his teeth now, but he had to salvage what he could to save face. "See that you do, I expect to have it here within 48 hours Frank or our Chief of defense will be talking to your government about a different matter altogether. Catch my drift, Frank?"

Dell hung up. Dell picked up the phone once more and called Opal.

"This better be legit otherwise it's both of our asses on the line. This is your one favor Opal you have 72 hours to prove to the president your theory. And we will have the tech in 48hrs so I want to make crystal clear that if anything goes wrong the president will have you taken out. He cannot afford to go to war with America over something we have no proof of. So, I hope you are right."

Dell didn't wait for a response and hung up from the encrypted phone line.

Opal hung up and threw the phone in her kitchen sink and turned the water on. Part one of the plan was done now to wait for Ruby's part in all this.

CHAPTER 55

Brad packed a weekend bag and put it at the hallway door. He gathered some food and things he would need to keep him busy at the cabin. His area had not been touched by fire yet, but he was worried, nonetheless.

A soft knock on the door startled him as he looked through the peephole and saw Charlie had arrived and was nervously biting his fingernail while he waited for him to open the door. "Well, if it isn't trouble come in." Brad didn't see that Onyx was standing behind Charlie when he invited him in.

"Um, who is this then, another one of your thugs following you, Charlie?" Brad was in no mood not 24hrs ago the dog killed a man and he had never been so scared in his life.

"I am sorry for the intrusion, but I want you to meet Onyx. He and I are neighbors and..."

"This is no time for pleasantries Charlie! Excuse us for a moment." He grabbed him by the arm and quickly threw him in the bedroom and slammed the door behind him.

Charlie gasped. "OH shit, what happened here!"

"SHHHH! I don't know I thought you could tell me." Brad avoided looking down as he did not want to throw up again.

"I've put you in danger, you can't stay here. We have to leave here now!" Charlie was frantic. "I will explain more in the car, but I don't trust your place for listening ears, so we need to go. And don't worry about my friend we will drop him off on the way back and go from there."

Charlie opened the bedroom door and Onyx had Gizmo in his arms cradled like a baby rubbing him under his chin.

"We need to leave now. I will explain in the car." Charlie looked pale.

The front door burst open, and two men all dressed in black with full tactical gear on rushed into Brad's living room and into the hallway where the three men were standing.

"Get behind me!" Onyx gave the dog to Charlie as he flexed his arms in anticipation of a fight.

The men had Taser guns and clubs and came at Onyx. Onyx's arms turned black and glistened as his fist connected with the man in the helmet and instantly broke his jaw making the man go down on his knees holding his broken face.

The man behind him tasered him but the electric jolts did nothing but amplify his strength as the blue electric lights vibrated around his biceps like a loose bracelet. He removed them from his shirt and smiled at the armed man and punched him in the nose. The crack from the break was loud and made Brad cringe. It sent the man to the floor holding on to what was left of his face.

Onyx looked back at them and put his finger to his lips to signal for them to be quiet.

Sirens were in the distant background now and time was running short. Onyx scanned for more men but didn't see any. He looked out the front step and a few people across the street in their homes were looking through the curtains.

"Let's go quickly," Onyx said as he stepped outside.

Once away from the house Charlie began to tell him about the recent events leading up to this point.

"I must apologize for being curt with you, I am missing my girls, and I am afraid something bad has happened to them. And, after that man came into my home I have been out of sorts. I am glad she reached out to you.

"Onyx, I apologize to you as well for not realizing that you are a distant relative, and I should have realized when I heard your name. But as you can see it has been a nightmare ever since my girls left for Madagascar." Brad stroked Gizmo who was on his lap in the backseat.

"No need for apologies Brad. It's been difficult for all of us. I am just glad that we showed up when we did to aid you out of there. We need to stick together now and find Ruby and Diamond." Onyx looked out the window and felt a growing worry within him.

CHAPTER 56

Ruby was out of the cavern and had taken Opal's car after she dropped her back at the beach. It wasn't worth both of them getting caught she needed to do this alone for her sister and for all of those who passed away because of what she started.

She drove into a busy part of downtown and parked her car. The plan had to work it just had to. She waited for signs from government officials but saw nothing yet. She decided to get something to eat and ventured out for a burger as her stomach was giving her grief and making so much noise it was becoming increasingly distracting.

As she ate the best burger she ever had, or it was the hunger talking she thought about Diamond and the last moments. She saw that man's face who was pointing the gun at them. Forever imprinted in her mind as he pulled the trigger, she could see it all in slow motion and realized it was too late long before she gathered enough energy to take them away from there.

A single tear fell from her eye as she wiped it, she looked up from her windshield of the car and saw that very same man in plain clothing walk by her car. He looked straight at her as if to provoke her out of the vehicle.

She threw her burger out the side window and opened the car door forgetting the plan altogether and needing retribution for her sister she became enraged with anger. Her hands vibrated as she walked behind him. People freaked and scattered to walk across the street to avoid her glowing arms.

She couldn't control herself she wanted him to pay. She grabbed him by the shoulder. Upon her turning him around he had a weapon of his own which he shoved into her stomach. Before she knew what had taken place the man grabbed her, and other men were now on top of her. Trapped and in pain, she tried to fight them.

She burned some of them who tried to put handcuffs on her. She briefly got away. She staggered and managed to push one of them about four feet into the air before she fell on the ground holding her stomach.

The men waited with shields and approached her. They didn't touch her at first but poked her with their batons. She couldn't hear what they were saying as she was fading out of consciousness. The last face she saw was lifting her before she blacked out.

Hours later she woke up and found she was bound to a hospital bed. It wasn't ordinary straps but a chemical compound that withstood the heat. She looked at it and tried to set herself free with no luck. Terrified, she looked around. A heart monitor was hooked up to her and her stomach was bandaged up. She started to feel the pain of it again. It was excruciating. She didn't have the strength to self-heal even though she was unable to reach the wound.

She realized that her arm was exposed, and it revealed her gem on her bicep in the hospital gown that she was now wearing. She looked towards the door and saw an officer was blocking the exit. What would they do to her if all her fears were now a reality? The thoughts were overwhelming, and she blacked out again.

CHAPTER 57

"Good work John, for putting inside agents in Australia right away before they detected who they were. We were not about to deploy our men out and risk losing something so valuable. Once the president sees what they have they will understand why we had to step in, and we will be the heroes."

Frank had finally won one he thought. Now they would be able to find out how she works and get more information about them.

"We need to make sure that our package will be transferred back to California safely. But we need the Australian government's help and cooperation to do that Frank. I am not sure who you want me to call to make that happen."

John took no pride in breaking the laws and was sure to be reprimanded by higher-ranking officers once it was all said and done. Perhaps even lose his job if this didn't go the right way. He was secretly hoping they would. He was tired of the games and hurting people to get what they wanted.

"Leave that to me. I will call Dell and by now he should have the data and all the scientific proof he needs so I'm sure it will go smoothly."

Frank was confident that the facts would speak for themselves. Frank left the office and phoned Dell in his car on the way home. It had been a long week, and he was glad to get home at a decent hour.

"Well, I take it you have everything we sent you? Sorry about interfering but as you can see it was for the good of the country on both sides wouldn't you agree?"

"No, I would not. And the president is not happy either Frank. We had an agreement. You violated that agreement and consider this our last conversation as you have now been fired from your president for taking this matter into your own hands."

Dell hung up. Frank stared into his cellphone with disbelief. The next phone call that came upon his phone was an unknown number. Frank was indeed fired and stripped of ranking from the secret service. Frank did not get a word in edgewise as he listened, he was yelled at by the American national secretary of defense.

He was to be arrested at once or turn himself in and state that he worked on his own without the American government backing him up. John would be taking over his position as of now. He was the secret service head of department facilitator. That was the end of Frank's career.

CHAPTER 58

Andry recovered while the boat sailed towards America. His burns were now scary as he looked off into the choppy water and thought about his son and how he missed him so. The Jamaican government dubbed him a hero and thanked him for saving the people on the bus that day. He was welcomed to come back when everything was back to normal. He would visit again.

The ship docked by the California shores, and he gathered his belongings and walked off the deck to find Ruby and hopefully settle all this mess. He had no idea how he would find her or if he ever would, but he had to try. He made a promise a long time ago and he aimed to keep it.

"Ruby I hope I find you soon and all will be fixed," Andry said as he walked over to a bunch of parked taxi drivers who would take him to a nearby motel for the night. Hopefully, he could get some information from the locals. He was hopeful and knew it would all work out somehow. The taxi driver proved to be quite knowledgeable about how to find someone. He would ask around as well and took his number where he was staying. Most of the conversation was about how terrible the weather was, and everyone thought the world was coming to an end.

Andry hoped it wasn't he that had the stone in his bag and held on to it tightly. He waved the taxi goodbye and went to his motel. It was late now, and tomorrow was a big day. He turned on the television as he sat and ate pizza take out and saw Ruby on the news. He dropped his slice of pizza and turned up the volume.

"In world news today a strange sighting in Australia as a woman attacked a man whose hands had appeared to be glowing. The men then forcibly attacked the woman, and she is now in hospital. Since she is an American citizen, the government will be transferring her to a secure location within the next few days to undergo testing and analysis as to why this happened. Sounds like something from the Avengers, back to you Steve."

Andry couldn't believe it. What was Ruby doing in Australia? He thought to himself. He was glad they were bringing her back, but he would have to figure out a way to stop them from doing tests on her. Andry took out the stone once more and looked at it closely. He had no idea how this stone was going to change anything, but he had to try and get this to her.

CHAPTER 60

In the heart of the concealed cave, Opal and Jade were shrouded in an unsettling silence, haunted by the absence of communication from their companion for a harrowing 24 hours. The passage of time contradicted their expectations, intensifying Opal's growing concern for their missing ally.

Unable to contain her restlessness, Opal rose from her seat, the echoes of her footsteps magnifying the tension in the cave. Jade, sensing Opal's escalating distress, extended a comforting hand.

"There was some delay, and the phone call did indeed work. Then she would have no reason for her to be a decoy, right? If you want, I can check on her and see with my mind. Just know that it will only be to make sure she's okay."

"Oh please, it would put my mind at ease. I know what Dell promised but you never know. I would feel better if I knew she was okay."

"I will have to rest afterward however it is quite draining for me at my age and what with all that is happening."

Jade closed her eyes, and her arm began to glow steadily. Within seconds her eyes opened wide.

"They have taken her. She is hurt. Opal, you must go to her and help! Quickly!!"

Opal didn't hesitate she ran full speed back out of the cave out into the open water where the entrance was. The wind had picked up and was making the waves over five feet high. It crashed into her, and she lost her balance struggling to get back to the shore.

She got swept up in the waves a few times before finally reaching the shore soaked and tired, she got up and ran as fast as her legs could carry her to the payphone. She called for a taxi to take her to Dell's home.

She got in the cab and the driver was annoyed she was wetting his seats. She told him it was an emergency, and she would cover the cost of the clean including the fare but 'for the love of god hurry up and drive!'

It was pouring rain now and the wind was fierce. Tree branches hit the taxi and bounced off crashing into the parked cars on Dell's street. The taxi driver made a corny joke as she opened the door to leave.

"Eh well, at least you don't have to worry about getting wet in the rain, eh?"

The bald man in his sixties with an Italian accent chuckled. Opal slammed the door, ran up to the porch, and rang the doorbell.

"What in the world are you doing here, Opal?"

Dell's expression on his face said it all. He was not expecting to ever see her at his door.

Opal went in without an invitation she was soaked once more and dripping all over his marble flooring. "I am so, sorry to barge in like this but I have to ask you something. The woman they took into custody that's American what hospital is she in?"

"You could have called. I know you're a bleeding heart, but this is ridiculous. She is the property of the Americans now we have no rights to her only that she will be removed, and the issue will be taken up with the secret service. And, you have yet to prove she has something to do with the weather." Opal frowned.

"Have you looked outside, Dell? More importantly, have you been following the news? The weather phenomenon is because of those people that have been chasing out of their areas. Listen I don't want to sound crazy, but you have to trust me."

"One second, I have to take this phone call. The president is up in arms with the American embassy about this woman and he is not convinced but trusts you because of how much work you have done for him."

Dell turned around and walked out of earshot while he took the call. Opal started to shiver. Dell, while on the phone turned around and looked at Opal.

"I see. Yes, she is here. I will do my best Mr. President."

He hung up the phone and went to his drawer in the foyer and took out a metal object. Before Opal recognized what it was, he was pointing it at her.

"Nice and slow Opal and no one gets hurt. I am under direct orders to keep you here while the secret service picks you up. Now I see why you have so much interest in that woman. You are one of them. You realize now that you will be considered a spy, and they will imprison you. What exactly are you?"

"Dell, how long have you known me for? Do I look like a spy to you? Yes, I am one of them, but we have no intention of hurting anyone, it's the exact opposite. Please let me leave and I promise you I will fix this."

Opal started going back up to the door. Her hand was fiddling with the doorknob.

"I have my orders. Explain to me what you are and why she is here?" Dell stepped closer and opal knew he was good at managing a gun, so she put her hands up above her head.

"I am not that different from you. We are called Lapillus Populus. We protect the land in which we were born with the help of the stones of the earth. I know you won't believe me so if you let me show you my arm, I will prove it to you."

Opal slowly put her arms down. Dell took a quick step closer, and the gun was under her chin. "Show me, no funny business, or I will shoot you."

Opal lifted her soaked sleeve to reveal her Opal stone inserted in her left bicep. It glowed like a rainbow. Dell gasped. He put the gun down and put his hand on his cheek in disbelief.

"Damn. This is madness."

He looked at Opal's expression and saw her for whom she was not a monster but as an extraordinary being.

"I have always considered you like a sister and now this. I have no words to express this utter and complete shock..." his voice trailed off.

"Let me go, Dell. Please. I need to save her. She belongs free in her own country living her life, not in a lab being probed. Same with me, don't I deserve to live my life?" Opal pleaded with his kind heart.

Dell put the gun up once more and pointed it to her face. "I cannot let you go. I am sorry but I have my orders. If you are innocent, they will let you go."

"You believe that?"

"If you say to them what you told me then everything will be fine. You can't run from them. They will hunt you down and shoot first. At least now you have a chance to explain it all to them."

"You are blind to the realities of how people treat anyone different than them. We see it every day the racism the hatred for anything that isn't exactly like them. They will kill her and me."

Opal had no choice now time was running out. Her arms started to glow white, and the rest of her body followed suit.

"What are you doing? Stop that!" Dell yelled out.

CHAPTER 61

The three men were quiet for most of the ride. They kept the radio off and sat in silence. Charlie stopped at a roadside dinner and parked the car.

"Listen I think we need to keep our strength. We don't know what we are going to be going up against. Well, if it's anything like the men back at the house am sure there will be more. Let's just get something to eat and unwind for a bit. Then we can drive into the next town. No one has been following us but just to make sure if they are we will be able to spot them once we start driving again." Charlie spoke as he shut off the car.

Both men mumbled they were hungry also and Brad decided not to leave Gizmo in the car and emptied his gym bag and put him inside zipping him inside but with only his head sticking out. They sat in the dingy rundown restaurant and ordered food and coffee. It was going to be a long drive to the next town, and they needed to stay alert. Gizmo was fed bits of everyone's meals, and he was happy about that. Brad looked over at the

TV that was facing them and saw a picture of his daughter on the news.

"Can you turn that up?" he looked at the men as Charlie went pale as he recognized her also. The waitress turned it up since there were just them in the restaurant anyway and left to grab a smoke outback.

"Oh my god!" Charlie was the first to speak.

Brad's eyes filled with tears. "It's come to this. My angel, what have they done to you."

Onyx didn't know who they were talking about until they said her name. He understood they were all in danger now.

Charlie looked at Brad. "They are bringing her home at least then we can get her."

"It won't be easy since they want to know how she works, and it will be only a matter of time before they capture every one of us and dice us up to see what makes us tick." Onyx was very dark but truthful. He was scared, this had never happened before, and he didn't know how they would be able to run from them.

Brad pet Gizmo and gathered his thoughts. "Everything will work itself out. It has to. We just need to show them that we are harmless, and we are there as protectors and healers, not the freaks that the media is trying to portray."

"I hope you are right. I need her to be alright. I think I am in love with your daughter." Charlie blushed as he looked at Brad with tear-filled eyes.

"Well, then we better save her and fix this because I hope she feels the same for you." Brad patted him on the back as they walked back to the car.

Onyx smiled at Charlie. "Let's go save your lady!" he lightly teased Charlie as he started up the car again.

With the distraction of the news, they had forgotten to keep an eye out for anyone following them. Two black SUV bulletproof vehicles kept a distance of two kilometers back to ensure they were not going to be spotted. Four men in each vehicle were armed with guns in hand and ready to apprehend them when they got the all-clear.

By the time they had arrived at the motel, it was midnight. The men got a room and settled in for the night. It had been a long eventful day and who knew what other surprises were in store for them. They could not afford to be tired. The black SUV pulled up into the gravel parking lot and the officer called John to wait for orders.

"I want to make sure we have them by surprise. Wait another hour and then break into the room. Leave no escape route untouched. I want those men back here at headquarters for interrogation." John spoke with the authority of his new position which he didn't want but the pay was good.

"Yes, sir, we will contain them." The young officer just on the force and wanting to prove himself answered. Sam was his name, and he was full of ambition. Recently graduated and top in his class. His boots were shining, and his hair placed just so. He was made for this job. He loved the action and was thrilled to be called on for his first assignment so soon. He stood six feet tall and looked more like a tree trunk than a man.

One hour passed. Sam told three men to go around back and make sure no one left. He took three men with him and told the other officer to make sure no one came out on the second floor as witnesses. Sam kicked in the door and the flashlights were on the men sleeping.

"You are all under the property of the government you are coming with us. Make no sudden movements or we will be forced to shoot you. Put your hands in the air!"

Gizmo barked and accidentally peed himself at the loud men who startled him awake. Brad put his hands up and obeyed them. Onyx on the other hand had other ideas. In the dark, they couldn't quite make out his arms and entire body turning black and as slick as tar. He was invisible as the men shone the flashlight on Brad and Charlie.

He slipped onto the floor and hid behind Sam as he got his handcuffs out to put on Brad. Onyx was lightning fast. He kicked Sam's legs out from beneath him and he fell. The other two officers shone a light on the area behind him and saw nothing but blackness.

One of the men put the gun up to Charlie's head and Spoke out loud not knowing where Onyx was.

"I will shoot him if you do not reveal yourself. Show yourself!" The man's voice broke showing some sign of fear.

Onyx could see the other men approaching so he had to act fast. He grabbed the man behind and threw him at the three approaching men. They all felt like bowling ball pins. They scrambled to get up as Charlie backed up near the entrance of the doorway. The Officer still had his gun pointing at Charlie.

"Where do you think you're going?" Charlie lifted his arms and stopped moving.

Onyx was slithering along the black wall sure to not be seen by the motel sign that was reflecting in. He went under the bed like an eel it was as if he was hovering cause the movements were so light that no one would have known he was there that fast if he was a human.

He was now behind the man with the gun. His hand reached out and grabbed it from him heating the metal just enough to burn the man's hands to release it. Charlie ran out the front door and toward his parked car. Onyx held the gun to the officers now standing up.

"Brad, you must go, now! Don't look back."

Onyx did not want to hurt them, but he knew they would hurt him. He pointed it at the officers, and they raised their hands. The men's eyes were wide with amazement seeing this black figure pointing the gun at them. Brad gathered gizmo up in his arms and followed Charlie out the door.

No sooner were they outside than they heard an officer tell them to put their hands up. They looked around and saw no one at first until they looked up and saw that one of the officers was on the second floor and pointing a large gun at them.

Charlie dropped to his knees and put his hands up. Brad held on to Gizmo and with one free hand, he put it up and stood beside Charlie. They were caught. Onyx came out of the motel with the gun still pointing at the officers inside. He saw the two of them with their hands up. Onyx decided now he had no choice but to leave them. He stayed black and blended in with the shadows and ran off to the wooded area out back. The officers put the handcuffs on the men and put them into the SUV.

"Two out of three isn't bad right?" One of the men spoke jokingly.

Sam was annoyed whatever that thing was it got the best of him. "No, it's bad. I have one of the energy readers so drop me off here and I am going to pursue him on foot. He can't escape we will find him."

The driver pulled off the highway and let Sam out. He went into the bush with his black night vision goggles and an aka47 in pursuit of the freak as he called it.

CHAPTER 62

Ruby felt movement as she stirred awake still groggy from the medication, they had given her. Eight army officers were surrounding her moving hospital bed. One nurse was pushing the bag of medicine attached to her arm. The lights from the hospital were too bright so she squinted as she tried to get answers.

"Where..." she cleared her dry throat. "Where are you taking me?"

No one answered her they just kept walking. She tried to move her arm and realized she was still tied to the bed and her feet were as well.

"HEY, someone, answer me! what are you doing with me, where are we going?"

One of the officers looked over at her and looked at some paperwork.

"Home."

She struggled to move and felt the pain from the stab wound in her stomach. She could have healed herself if she could reach it. They didn't speak to her for the entire ride back. The man looked at her medication bag and then looked away at his book he was reading ignoring Ruby who had asked for a drink of water.

Once the flight touched down the officers were ready to receive Ruby and exchange paperwork. Ruby looked at the man who was talking and recognized him. He was one of the men who were at the beach that night. The night they took her sister, and her arms began to glow, and her entire body heated up as the man looked over at her and saw her fight to get free.

"Hey, now we are not going to fight you, little lady. Just calm down we are taking you to get medical care for your wounds to make sure they did a good job of mending you. Relax we will be there soon little lady."

The man grinned. Ruby became enraged, even now hearing his voice made her want to rip out his throat. The pain of the stitches in her stomach started to pull as she fought against the hospital bed.

A nurse was called, and she came over with a needle and jabbed it in her shoulder before she could get a chance to break free. The bars on the bed were warped from the strength of her but since they had still drugged her so much, she didn't have enough strength to break free. The man was surprised she was even awake since they had given her a sedative for the flight home.

Within seconds she was knocked out. They took her by helicopter to the California Science and Environmental facility which was nowhere near the hospital. John was waiting for her, and scientists were setting up testing to figure out how she worked and if they could harness her powers.

CHAPTER 63

Opal didn't want to hurt Dell, but she had no choice, everything was falling apart. She attacked him viciously grabbed a hold of his gun as it went off and threw it on the ground. Her nails dug into Dell's skull as she fought him.

He was a black belt in karate and kicked opal as hard as he could which knocked her over and hit the banister that was in the front foyer. She grabbed the railing and yanked on it which snapped it partway and she hit him with the metal end in the face. He got hit once but ducked the second time and managed to hit her in the back and the pain was blinding.

She nearly got kicked again while she was on the ground but managed to roll away in time. She grabbed his leg and launched him. She threw him into the front doors sending it breaking and splitting into many pieces as the wood and glass broke.

It knocked him out. She had to be sure he wouldn't follow her, so she went over and with a piece of glass that had broken off, she stabbed him in the chest. The sirens were getting louder now. They would be coming for her. She ran as fast as she could to get away from the area knowing full well, they would be able to track her. The only refuge now was the cavern where Jade was safe and to risk putting her in danger, she couldn't do it.

She jumped over fences and into people's backyards. People screamed as she jumped from one end to another never looking back. She turned the corner into an alleyway and misguided her whereabouts and ended up in a dead-end. She looked back and didn't hear anything and decided to go a different way.

A black sedan screeched to a Holt and stopped right at the entrance of the alley. She was trapped. They found her and now all was lost. Opal was not going down without a fight. Everyone was dying and she knew they would never let her go. The men got out of the vehicle and pointed their guns at her.

"Put your hands up and come quietly. You know we will find you wherever you go so there isn't any sense in running anymore Opal."

Opal spat on the ground and started to glow. Her entire body lit up it was a blinding white light. The men had a hard time looking at it because it was like looking into the sun. The walls of the alleyway shook with the amount of power Opal was emanating.

"Come and get me, boys!" Opal smiled if she was going down, she was going to at least have fun.

The men went into the alleyway and sounds of guns went off as they were too blinded by her light to see her directly. She used it to her advantage and kicked one of the officer's knees which dislocated it and sent him to the ground. She grabbed his gun as he let it go to hold his knee in pain as he fell.

She pointed it at the officer behind him and didn't hesitate. She pulled the trigger and shot him in the chest. The other officer was behind the vehicle and aimed in the direction of the light and fired until the light went out.

The weather network issued a warning for Australia they were in for a major disaster. Three hurricanes were approaching as if out of nowhere and it was gauged at a category 5 one of the worst in history that they had ever had.

Thousands of people ran from their businesses in a frantic panic to get home and away from the water as there was little time. They had little warning and now the people were going to die. Cars jammed streets as overcrowding and panic-stricken people got out of their cars and began to run on foot inland.

Jade was safe deep within the cavern hidden in the middle of the earth's core. She felt Opal's life and tears fell from her eyes as another light was snuffed out. She closed her eyes and fell for Ruby. She was still alive but weak and drugged. She called out to her in her mind to be strong and fight. It was up to Ruby now to save that world before it was too late.

She could feel the world's fear and the dangers that were happening globally. Jade went to the walls covered in stones and felt them with her hands. A light flickered in them as she touched it.

CHAPTER 64

Andry parked his rental outside of the science and environmental facility it was fenced and gated. Security was tight and men with guns were patrolling the inside of the facility. The stone sat in the front seat of his car. He scanned the area for any signs of Ruby. He didn't see any.

He waited for hours as three black SUV sedans pulled up to the gate. The Security officers ushered them in. Andry strained to get a good look at the people coming out of the vehicles. He kept looking squinting his eyes to see it looked as though it was only a bunch of officers at first, but two civilians handcuffed finally got out of the back seat and were escorted to the entrance of the building. He spotted a dog in one of the man's hands. He was an older gentleman.

Andry got out of the car and took his backpack with him. He hid behind the bushes near the left side of the entrance to get a better view and see if he could hear anything. Just then another three black SUV sedans a van and a police escort pulled up with the lights on but no siren. The police car pulled off to the side and allowed the vehicles to go ahead once the gate was opened.

It had to be her he thought. He wanted to get a bit closer and accidentally stepped on a branch and it broke making a loud noise. The armed men heard it but didn't come over to investigate it since they were preoccupied. He froze nonetheless and waited hoping he would see Ruby.

The men who were guarding the fenced area were now pointing the gun at the back of the van. Ruby busted out of the van and the doors flew off hitting them. She was wearing a nightgown from the hospital and looked wild and crazy as her red body tossed the men easily away from her. She disappeared back into the van, and it screeched backward as the gunmen got up being run over by the van.

Ruby was driving and she did not put on the brakes to stop at the closed gates. She busted through and smashed the gates open with the van which cracked the windshield. More men poured out of the building and ran to the vehicles in pursuit of Ruby.

She drove down the road at full speed and misjudged the turn and the van tipped to its side as she drove on two wheels. She made the corner nearly losing control of the van as it slammed

back down on the ground. The police car and sedans were just heading out the parking lot when
Andry decided now would be the best time to run
back to the car and follow them.

He turned right into an officer's gun. "What
are you doing here? You shouldn't be hiding in
the bush civilian. Move along before I arrest you
for trespassing."

Andry pretended he didn't speak English.
Said something in his native tongue and walked
down the street away from his car and the entrance of the building. He walked for a short while
and came across a restaurant and decided it was
best to wait it out before going back to his car.

Ruby was on the highway now and more
and more police officers had been dispatched to
stop her. She was weaving in and out of traffic.
The medical supplies had slowly been falling out
of the back of the van and leaving a mess of traffic
behind her.

Ruby was not even sure where she was going but far away from them. There was a cellphone in the cupholder. She reached for it and
dialed Charlie's cell. No answer. She looked down
and tried to call her father not paying attention to

the tractor-trailer that was pulling out of the slow lane in front of her.

Before she could respond and slam on the breaks, she went into the back of the tractor with the van causing it to jackknife and cars were honking and slamming on their brakes hitting the tractor. Ruby was thrown from her seat and catapulted through the windshield and went into the side of the tractor with her body. She was glowing red still which gave her protection and melted the metal container instantly and she landed on the crates inside of it just barely scrapping her leg as she entered.

The police and the agents were stuck in the mess of traffic the accident had caused which forced them to go on foot. John was in the vehicle and was amazed at what he saw.

"Listen we need to go slow here don't startle her. The last thing we need is more deaths and civilian casualties do you hear me? Keep the gun close but don't show it."

He got out of the vehicle and left the door open as she slowly walked and weaved through the wreckage to get close enough to talk to her.

"Ruby, we are not here to harm you," John spoke softly. "Can we just talk? We want to know about you and your kind we want to understand you. Please no more violence."

Ruby got out of the back of the mangled trailer and looked him dead in the eye. "Now you want to talk. You kill my sister chase me all over the world and now you want to talk?" Ruby folded her arms and looked around as the other officers approached.

"So why do you need all these men with guns if you just want to talk? Do you think I am that stupid? You don't want to tell you just want to dissect me and see what makes me tick like I'm some kind of genetic mutant. You will never understand because you don't want to know the truth you just want to take what I have." Ruby jumped down still glowing red, but she seemed to have died down since her legs and shoulders were now back to human.

John thought about it and spoke. "You were right. Those men who were in charge of this operation did just want that, but I am now in command, and I don't. I want to help, let's figure this out together. Come back with me and I will make sure they don't harm you further. We have your father I am sure he will want to see you."

Ruby's eyes opened wide while grinding her teeth. "What do you want with my father? He has nothing to do with this. It was my mother who... you need to release him. He doesn't have powers as I do so he cannot help you anyway."

Ruby went completely red again her heart sank as she felt completely trapped yet again and another person she loved was in danger.

John took a step back from her. "No harm will come to him but we don't know he isn't like you as it stands and so we will keep him with us for safekeeping."

Ruby screamed in frustration putting all her strength into the cry, and it was so loud that it burst some of the windshields of the crashed cars surrounding her.

Ruby glowed fully once more. "I will not be made to bend because of the likes of you. But I forewarn you leader of this hunting game you have going for my family and my kind. I will find you and I will kill you if you touch a hair on his head or any other of us." Ruby looked over at a clearing and ran for it.

John ran after her but was not fast enough to catch her. His walkie-talkie went off asking for clearance to shoot her. He threw it into the ground and smashed it to pieces. He couldn't keep up with her she was too fast.

He let her go and knew he would find her again.

He called after her, "There's no where you can run, I will find you. Until we meet again."

CHAPTER 65

Sam went into the farm field which was full of corn higher than him. He knew he was hiding somewhere amongst it so he started talking loudly so Onyx could hear him.

"Hey freak! You are causing a lot more problems for yourself not coming quietly. Now we can charge you with failing arrest and under suspicion of supernatural Hocus Pokus. Eh, freak?"

He kept treading into the cornfield deeper and deeper.

"Come out and play, freak! I got something here that you won't be able to get through this here gun in my hand."

Onyx heard him off in the distance and he decided to wait for him to come to him. It was now dawn and the sun was starting to rise. Onyx only had a little time left before he would be seen again. Sam crept silently and softly crouched down as he saw some movement up ahead of him. He fell silent and put the gun out in front of him and took the safety off his gun.

Onyx watched him and decided to taunt him a little first by moving the corn and then dashing to the left of it. Sam fell for it and followed making him in front of Onyx now. Onyx didn't hesitate he blindly attacked and took the gun out of Sam's hand before he punched him in the eye socket. Then Onyx put the gun in front of Sam's face and pointed it at him.

"Well, well, looks like the big talker is getting a piece of his own medicine."

"Eh don't point that thing at me if you don't know how to use it freak." Sam wasn't intimidated.

"Oh, you mean like this?" and he shot him in the foot.

Sam went down with a thud. "You freak! You will pay for that. I will hunt you down and find you again mark my words!" He was gripping his boot with a bullet hole now oozing a lot of blood.

"Well in that case I better keep this gun for you for next time." Onyx laughed took his

cellphone he had in his front pocket and disappeared into the cornfield a different way and left
Sam to hold his foot.

CHAPTER 66

Andry waited a few hours before returning to grab his car. He approached with caution but didn't see any of the men who were patrolling the gates. He quickly got in his car and drove off in the direction of Ruby's last moments.

He couldn't believe his eye the highway had been closed and police tape was seen in the area. Officers had scanners and were standing around talking to civilians. Andry decided to take the back road and see if he could find her.

He drove for a couple of miles and spotted a shadow of a figure up ahead walking off the side of the shoulder on the gravel road. He figured it must be her. He sped up and realized when he got closer it was a man. The man waved him down. Andry unrolled his window and slowed to get on to the shoulder.

"Hi sorry to bother you but would it be possible to hitch a ride to the nearest phone I need to locate someone." Onyx put her hands on the car door throwing her head right into the opened window.

"Sure, I am looking for someone myself so hop in." Andry had a good feeling about this man despite his tall stature his eyes looked kind.

"Thanks so much, man." He got in and put on his seat belt.

They drove for a few miles and still nothing. Onyx was curious about his accent, so he decided to strike up a conversation. "You don't sound like you are from around these parts. My name is Onyx. I hope you don't mind a little conversation I need to stay awake." He chuckled.

"Ah, I don't mind. I am not from here I am from an island off the coast of Madagascar. I am just here visiting a friend who lives here but I can't seem to find her. I should have called first. Onyx is your name. Huh, my friend's name is also after a stone Ruby." Andry had already put it together when he mentioned his name. He knew he was in good company.

"NO WAY! Are you kidding? What are the odds! Unbelievable! My buddy I need to call is sweet on a woman named Ruby, too. Yeah, we got separated back at the hotel and I'm hoping he's ok." Onyx wasn't sure just how much information he should be giving away.

Andry slowed the vehicle down and pulled it over. "Can you describe her to me? It is the same person if you don't mind."

After describing her to Andry he was convinced it was her. He told her that he helped her get something deep in the caves that was very important. Onyx knew what he was talking about and divulged the story up until this point.

Andry was pleased to have found him. "I am a firm believer that things always come together just as the universe had intended. I can now show this to you know what is supposed to be done with it and how it can help." Andry grabbed his bag and showed Onyx the stone.

Onyx was beyond delighted when he saw the stone. "Ruby has to grind this stone and drink it. She will have immense powers so much so that no one has ever known before. It has never been done before mixing the stones, but the Mystical **Powers** of **Alexandrite** is believed to bring balance in the interaction between the physical manifest world and the manifest spiritual or astral world. It opens the crown chakra, bringing one access to the warm, healing energy and love of the universe. With the Ruby within her will amplify its ability and restore the earth's life force as well."

"Amazing." Andry was speechless.

"We need to find her quickly. Let's keep driving and hopefully we can run into her." Andry was convinced this would be the answers they were looking for to put an end to all of it.

CHAPTER 67

Charlie and Brad found themselves confined in a dimly lit room; the air heavy with the scent of uncertainty. The sterile environment offered little comfort, and their predicament was worsened by the limited furnishings—a solitary table and two chairs. Gizmo, their loyal companion, paced restlessly, his anxious demeanor betraying a pressing need.

As Brad contemplated the intricacies of escape, the wheels turning in his mind, Charlie looked to alleviate Gizmo's tension. The minutes ticked by, and the tension mounted.

"Poor Gizmo, you don't care for that blingy collar, do you? It looks like you want to take it off, eh boy," observed Charlie, his eyes narrowing in thoughtful concern.

A spark of inspiration ignited in Brad's mind. "That's it! You are a genius, Charlie." Seizing Gizmo, he leaned in and whispered a mysterious directive into the pug's attentive ear.

Gizmo's eyes glowed an ethereal blue as he fixed his gaze on the door handle. A surreal transformation unfolded—the metal handle softened, yielding to an unseen force, and then began to liquefy, streaming down the door in a mesmerizing display of canine-induced alchemy.

"Holy hell! WOW, how the hell did he do that?" Charlie exclaimed; in shock with widened eyes.

"I will explain later; right now, we have to get out of here and far away from this place," Brad urged, urgency permeating his voice. Casting a cautious glance through the now-handle-less door, he assessed the hallway beyond. A moment of resolute determination passed, and he signaled for Charlie to follow as they slipped out and navigated the labyrinthine corridors.

Turning a corner, their hope of an unguarded exit was thwarted by the unexpected presence of formidable guards. The realization that their path to freedom was obstructed sent a ripple of tension through the air. The guards, stoic and imposing, stood as formidable sentinels, their gaze fixed on the intruders.

Charlie and Brad exchanged a wary glance, silently acknowledging the challenge that lay ahead.

"Here goes nothing," Charlie stood in the hallway and coughed loudly.

The men yelled out, "Hey, how did you get out of there?" They ran towards him.

"What kind of plan is that?" Brad asked as he hid behind the wall.

"Quick tell that dog whatever you said before to do that thing with his eyes again!" Charlie backed up.

Brad pointed at the men and whispered in his ear once more. The dog's eyes lit up and aimed at the men stopping them dead in their tracks. They ran back to avoid being hit by the blue beams that were burning everything in its path.

Brad kept moving forward as the men scrambled to get out of the way. The exit was clear, and the men had no choice but to let them go. Once outside Brad placed the dog on the ground and Gizmo ran to pee on the bit of grass by the fence.

"What did you say to him?" Charlie couldn't help but be curious.

"I told him if he needed to go pee he would have to get out of here because we were not allowed out." Brad chuckled. "I think it made him mad."

Charlie laughed. "Jeez, is that all? you should have told him that sooner."

Once out in the parking lot, they didn't have any followers, at least not yet. Charlie went to each vehicle to see if the keys were left in it. He found one finally after looking into four vehicles.

"Over here!" Charlie waved Brad over and Gizmo trotted behind him.

They left the parking lot, and it seemed a little too easy which was strange because before it was teeming with men with guns. Charlie drove and as they approached the highway seeing as it was closed knew that a lot of them were there. He took the back road, and they sighed a bit of relief for once he wasn't being followed.

They made it halfway towards another part of town before they spotted Ruby. She was obvious as she was wearing a hospital gown. Charlie pulled over and Brad got out of the van.

"Oh, my girl, what have they done to you. I missed you so much. I was so worried. Are you hurt?"

Brad became the worried dad instantly unraveling from the cool collected guy Charlie knew.

"Yes, I am okay dad. I healed my wounds. But I am afraid I have caused so much trouble and every one of us is in danger." Ruby buried her head into her father's chest and cried.

"There now, it will all be alright I know it will. You are stronger than this. Where is Diamond? I am surprised she is not with you." Brad looked at her as he rubbed her back.

"She's... she's gone."

Ruby's head dropped as she could not look him in the eyes. She gripped her father tighter as his heart sank. They all heard the helicopter off in the distance. Ruby jerked her head up.

"We need to go now."

Brad wiped his tears and got in the van after Ruby. Charlie smiled at Ruby although it was not the best time to.

"I see you two have met." Ruby sat in the backseat and fastened her seatbelt. Gizmo was ecstatic to see her and proceeded to lick her all over and jump on her lap.

"Yes, we have, it's a long story so we won't bore you with the details, but I think we are pretending to be good friends well enough." Charlie smiled in the rearview to look at Ruby. He was trying to lighten the mood but failing badly.

"Ha, funny guy, well, you are a decent man from what I gathered and decent enough to put yourself into this situation for me which I can never repay you. Plus seeing how you are here looking after my dad while I was gone." Ruby smiled back at him.

Brad was lost in thought and didn't join in the conversation.

"We need to formulate a plan before we have the government men on us again which by the looks of things will be soon." Charlie looked up to see if the helicopter was on top of them.

He wasn't paying attention to the road and swerved into the ditch.

"I don't know. They can find me wherever I go. They are tracking me with the energies I emanate so there is nowhere to hide. The only safe place was in Australia there was a cavern... but obviously, I can't get there now not with three people. It would be impossible."

"Well, let's keep driving and hopefully we can come up with something." Charlie was trying to be hopeful.

"I am starving. We should try to find somewhere to eat. I can think better with a full belly." Ruby thought out loud.

Brad looked at Charlie just then and they agreed.

"Well, if they find us at least we will have had a good meal," Brad said as he snapped out of his thoughts.

They all laughed. Nothing more they could do at that moment of desperation.

Andry and Onyx were stopped in a restaurant. They needed a break from looking for Ruby and needed to refuel. As they paid for the gas and grabbed some snacks for the road Charlie pulled up next to them. He didn't notice them at first as he climbed out of the black van. His back was turned to Onyx who was about to get into Andry's car when Charlie opened the door and nearly hit the car.

"Hey, man watch out," Onyx said as he saw the door swing open.

"Charlie, oh my god, I am ever glad to see you! Onyx went up to him and hugged him.

Charlie was equally surprised. "Onyx! You're alive!"

The men exchanged pats on the back and were happy to see one another considering the circumstances. Ruby stood there and watched them. "Um, this is a great family reunion. But I need to eat can we go inside please so I can get some food and you can chat amongst your-selves?" She smirked knowing that she was teas-ing them.

Onyx went up to Ruby and shook her hand. "Ruby it's so nice to finally meet Charlie's future wife." He elbowed Charlie as he went over to in-troduce himself.

Ruby gave Charlie a strange look with one eyebrow raised. "Hi there."

As soon as their hands connected, she felt a surge of relief and healing. He felt it too. They both stood for a while as the helicopter was now above them and five black sedans pulled into the parking lot.

Ruby felt recharged and rejuvenated. "Wow, thank you for that. I am restored and healed. I feel stronger than I have ever felt in my life."

Andry came out of the store and saw them all standing there. Ruby turned to see Andry.

She ran over and gave him a big hug. "What are you doing here? I didn't think I would ever see you again."

"I come bearing gifts. And it is just in time. Onyx did you, do it?" Andry looked over at him.

"Yes, I did it's here." He grabbed the cup from inside the car.

Andry looked at Ruby and looked her in the eyes. "There is no time to explain but you have to trust me okay. You must drink this. It is from your aunt. She told me if ever you were in dire need and danger that this would help."

Ruby did trust Andry and for the first time in her life there was no hesitation about who she was, and her heritage and she truly believed it would. The men were now outside the vehicles with guns. John was walking towards them with his hands up. The officers got out of the vehicles and watched with guns aimed at them.

"Ruby, we need to talk. You never let me finish what I needed to say. No one will hurt any of you, but I do need all of you to come with me now." John stopped fifteen feet away from where Ruby was standing.

The people in the restaurant were staring out the window. The clouds were swirling above them in an unforeseen force intertwined with webs of lightning. It had started to rain as the wind was picking up. Onyx handed the drink of grounded up Alexandrite that looked like a mix-ture of blue-green, purple sparkling liquid. Onyx had crushed it with his bare hands.

She held the cup out to john and gave a gesture of cheers and drank. Her body became red, but veins of the same color liquid could now be seen visibly throughout her entire body like a roadmap. The wind calmed and the sun came out.

An invisible pulse ejected from Ruby's body and expanded out to the world's farthest corners.

John stood and watched in awe as all the onlookers did in amazement as she transformed but it was more internal. The only thing to show this transformation was the permanent marking on the left and right sides of her neck which looked beautiful as if there were a mandala design on either side.

She looked at John and felt at peace. No anger no hate just empathy for those who didn't know any better. "I will talk to you alone. I have no issue with you or anyone. I want you to understand us."

She waved her hand out, and everywhere was filled with beauty. Flowers and trees and green pastures. Ruby was healing what the humans had done to destroy the environment. John stood back and looked in amazement. Onyx stood beside her, and Gizmo went by her side.

John looked at his energy scanner and couldn't believe his eyes. It was white. He hit it to see if it had glitches but nothing, but a white screen was all everyone saw. One of the officers took a step forward and pointed his gun. John saw him and told him to step back.

The man didn't listen. "This is an abomination! She needs to be destroyed."

"No!" John reached for his gun as the man kept walking closer to them.

Ruby didn't budge. She flared out her body liquefied dispersed into thin air and reappeared in front of him and with a blink of an eye disintegrated the man's gun simply by touching it turning it into dust before their very eyes.

Terrified, the man stepped back with his mouth agape.

Ruby looked at the other officers as they went ahead to drop their weapons and put their hands in front where she could see them. She smiled and reappeared with the others.

Back at the office, the devices stopped working all at once and no detection of energy irregularities could be found. It was as if the energy pulse had disabled all of the government equipment. The news alerts called off the hurricanes in Australia and everywhere the natural disasters had suddenly ceased.

John approached Ruby and shook her hand. His cellphone messages were ringing his phone off the hook. He talked to her in the restaurant as people stared at her while she ate.

"So, I think that we can put this to rest now. I am here as a guardian to protect the world from disasters and from destroying yourselves. You kill me or any of us, and this chain of events will happen again. The hurricanes. The volcanoes. Everything!" Ruby spoke as she ate her omelet.

John understood. He called the president at once and let her speak to him.

"I am glad we could work this out. I am out of a job now, but it was worth it. I didn't like it much anyway." John joked as the men pulled away and the helicopter gone ahead to leave.

"Well, you can open a new department to protect us from future dealings?" Ruby smiled at John as Charlie sat down beside her.

Brad and Onyx came in carrying Gizmo.

John got up and shook their hands. "No hard feelings fellas, just doing my job."

Onyx piped up. "Oh, there's an officer in a cornfield you may want to pick up with a bullet hole in his foot. Eh, no hard feelings." He smiled at John.

"Touché," John looked at Ruby as he walked out of the restaurant.

Ruby looked at the happy faces of everyone munching away and remembered Jade. "I have one more thing I have to do still."

And with that, she vanished in a cloud of colored smoke.

The men looked at each other and shrugged and continued to eat giving Gizmo a piece of bacon because he deserved it.

Within a few minutes, Ruby returned and sat down.

Charlie looked puzzled. "What did you have to finish?"

"I had to return a dear friend's home. But she decided she wanted to stay where she was, so I said my goodbyes." Ruby sat thinking about her passing. She was a lovely lady and would be missed.

"Oh," Charlie leaned over and kissed Ruby on the lips. Something he had wanted to do since he met her that day. Brad smiled and was happy for them. He knew Charlie was a decent man and went above and beyond for his daughter.

Onyx teased Charlie once more, "Hey, so, when is the wedding? *And* are you ever going drive me, back to my truck?"

They all laughed and realized the friendships that were made here that would last a lifetime.

Gizmo licked Ruby's face as she stroked his fur, she noticed his collar, "Mom, you would be so happy to see us, now."

About the Author

Lizy is a Canadian author, illustrator, and owner of The Elite Lizzard Publishing Company. She has written over 30 published books in different genres. She loves creating books that help kids and adults fall in love with reading!

Are you a fan? Get updates on new books by emailing elitelizzardpublishing@hotmail.com

If you liked this book, please leave a review.

www.ingramcontent.com/pod-product-compliance
Lightning Source LLC
Chambersburg PA
CBHW060355310726
48976CB00003B/834